Ever After High™

The Unfairest of Them All

BY SHANNON HALE

LITTLE, BROWN AND COMPANY

New York   Boston

Cover design by Tim Hall/Véronique Sweet.
Cover illustration by Antonio Javier Caparo.

Little, Brown and Company
Hachette Book Group
1290 Avenue of the Americas, New York, NY 10104
Visit us at LBYR.com
everafterhigh.com

Originally published in hardcover and ebook by
Little, Brown and Company in March 2014

First Paperback Edition: March 2018

Little, Brown and Company is a division of Hachette Book Group, Inc.
The Little, Brown name and logo are trademarks of Hachette Book Group, Inc.

The publisher is not responsible for websites (or their content)
that are not owned by the publisher.

Library of Congress Control Number 2013046320

ISBNs: 978-0-316-28202-4 (pbk.)

Printed in the United States of America

LSC-C

10 9 8 7 6 5 4 3 2 1

For Dinah and Wren, our little Royal and Rebel
(or is it the other way around?)

CONTENTS

A Very Evil
PROLOGUE

IF THE EVIL QUEEN HAD ONE WORD TO describe her living conditions, it would be *cramped*. If she had more than one word, she would add *intolerable*, *wretched*, and several others that well-trained Narrators choose to leave out of their tales.

Her cramped black glass cell was the *inside* of a magical mirror designed to hold only the greatest of terrors. Her eyes burned with violet flames at the memory of Milton Grimm and his petty magician pals ganging up to remove her from power.

To be fair, she *was* the Greatest Evil Ever After Has Ever Known. And not just for the poisoning-Snow-White bit, but also for the general rampaging that culminated in her invasion of Wonderland. But that Grimm couldn't be bothered to muster enough magical strength to form a cage worthy of her royal station still rankled. She swiped at the webs that grew from the cell's corners faster than she could destroy them, though she had never seen any spiders.

For what felt like the seventy-two thousandth time, she pressed her hand against the dirty-gray wall.

"Expand," she whispered.

"Enlarge," she spoke.

"Advance!" she shouted, and was immediately knocked onto her back by a wave of pain. She stood up shakily, fingers pinching the bridge of her nose. The headache would last a few hours, and then she would try again. The cell still wasn't any larger than before, but eventually she *would* find a weakness in the spell repellent—enough to expand her living space, if not to escape entirely.

Suddenly a burst of purple lightning ripped through the cell. She lifted her hands to cast an attack spell, but the lightning was already gone. She sniffed.

Something had changed. She wiggled her fingers in the air, feeling slightly less of a buzz than normal.

The Evil Queen held her hands in front of her, fingers forming a rectangle. She chanted:

> *A view, a sight, a clear crevasse*
> *A pass through glass of distance vast*
> *Become to find*
> *Form to show*
> *Whence did shine*
> *That lightning blow!*

Sweat beaded up on the Evil Queen's brow as pain lanced first through her head, her stomach, and then her left big toe. A rectangle of light traced itself into the wall in front of her. The light dimmed, leaving a two-foot-square wooden frame hanging on the wall.

"Ha-ha!" she shouted.

The spell repellent, though not gone, *had* lessened, enough to allow a little magic.

She began to hum. Silky fog snaked along the dark floor, up the wall. With a cracking sound that could only be described as the opposite of the noise a breaking window makes, the frame filled with silver glass. A real mirror at last! She inspected her face, noticing some of her black hairs had turned gray. She frowned and remembered that even her frown was beautiful.

With a few words and a flick of her hands (and a stabbing headache), the mirror's view deepened, and now she was spying through it onto the terrace court-yard of Ever After High. This was where the purple surge had come from?

A crowd on the terrace was in a panic. Children and teachers, mouths open in shock and terror. The queen couldn't help but smile. This was the sort of scene she found insanely funny. She spotted her daughter, Raven, standing high on the pedestal. The Evil Queen touched the glass.

"Rewind, design, reverse," she chanted. The view froze, and then events began to go backward, until she whispered, "Stop, stay, play." Now the mirror replayed the events of moments before. Raven was approaching a large book posted on the podium.

"Ah," the queen said. "It must be Legacy Day."

She rolled her eyes. It was a rite of passage for all the children of famous fairytales to sign the Story-book of Legends and bind themselves to repeating their parents' stories. Of course she wanted her daughter to become evil and follow in her own glorious footsteps. But true evil was doing what *you* wanted, for your own benefit, and this charade of Grimm's only served to reinforce *his* control.

But then, instead of signing her name, Raven tore her page out of the Storybook of Legends. The queen's clever eyes picked up a faint trace of purple magical energy blasting from the book. That answered one question. The magic that had been expelled when Raven tore her page rippled out, sending a shock wave even as far away as the mirror prison.

The queen paused the image and leaned in. Everyone in the crowd seemed afraid. Apple White, that daughter of her enemy, was about to burst into tears. But Raven stood tall on the pedestal, looking unrepentant. Powerful. So like her mother.

The queen's arms ached to hold the baby who had once fit there and the teenage daughter who was growing capable of shaking Ever After as much as her notorious mother did.

She smiled slowly, and then she began to laugh.

CHAPTER 1

A SPOONFUL OF PORRIDGE

MORNING ONCE-UPONED ALL OVER EVER After. Bluebirds sang, roosters crowed, and pixies buzzed in the Enchanted Forest.

Against the walls of the great Ever After High, sunrise glared red. All was still but for the Track and Shield students out for a morning run—pursued by a horde of screaming imps, Coach Gingerbreadman's latest tactic to get his team in shape.

In her dorm room, Apple White stood and stretched. Songbirds gathered on her windowsill and chirped a morning song. She smiled at them but couldn't muster a song of her own to whistle back.

She put on her most somber red skirt and white blouse and the very least shiny of her gold belts. She looked at her roommate from the corner of her eye. Raven Queen was sitting on her bed, head down, her long black-and-purple hair falling over her face as she tied the laces on her knee-high boots. She looked sad. Instinctively, Apple searched for something cheery to say, but the words caught in her throat.

Yesterday Raven Queen had managed to do the most evil thing ever. No, scratch that, *worse* than evil. She was *supposed* to be evil. What Raven had done was just straight-up selfish. When she didn't sign the Storybook of Legends—and worse, tore out her page—she royally messed up not only Apple's Happily Ever After but everyone else's, too. She and Raven were supposed to grow up and become the next Snow White and Evil Queen, just as their mothers had been. But if Raven refused to be evil, then Apple would never flee the dark and scary Queen Castle, meet the dwarves, eat a poisoned apple, and wake up to a prince's kiss.

Apple stared at her reflection in the mirror. She

could almost see her mother in that face, telling her, *Apple, you will fill the world with sunshine!* But how could she if her destiny was broken?

Suddenly, with a crash, something really did break.

Apple whirled to find her lounge throne—her favorite she'd had shipped from home—was in pieces. Draped over the pieces was Madeline Hatter. Her lavender-streaked teal hair exploded around her in messy curls. The polka-dotted, striped, and lacy layers of her skirt were bunched and fluffed. Her teacup hat tilted low over one ear.

"Whoops," Maddie said.

"Maddie!" Raven called out.

"Are you okay?" Apple asked as Raven helped their friend to her feet.

"I'm fine." Maddie picked up a chair leg. "But your poor chair. I smintered it all to pieces."

"Yes," Apple said, a little wistfully. "It's okay...but how—"

"It's okay?" Maddie examined another scrap of wood. "It doesn't look very okay. Is it supposed to come apart like this?"

"Apple means she isn't upset that you broke it, or at least she forgives you," Raven said.

Raven glanced uneasily at Apple.

"Oh, Raven," said Maddie. "I can hear an ache crouching behind your tongue. The kind of ache an empty cup has for honey and tea, or a white rabbit has for a proper waistcoat—"

"Maddie..." Raven looked down.

"And like I ache for breakfast!" said Maddie. "Breakfast cures most everything—except chairs. I'm sorry, Apple."

Maddie gave Apple a hug. She was shorter than Apple—one of the shortest girls in the school, and she stood on her toes to reach around her friend.

"I'll try to fix it later," said Maddie. "For now, we need to fix your empty stomachs. Let's all have breakfast together."

"Um..." said Apple, looking sideways at Raven.

"Er..." said Raven, peeking over at Apple. "I think Apple just needs some time to—"

"Excuse me?" said Apple. "You think *I* need time when you're the one who—"

"*Breakfast!*" Maddie declared. "Breakfast first, and then you two will be chatty and smiley again."

Maddie darted to their window, ready to leap. "Last one to the Castleteria is a rotten egg-man!"

"Whoa!" Apple said, grabbing Maddie's arm. "What are you doing?"

"We could get there way faster by jumping," Maddie said.

"We're, like, four stories up," Raven said.

"I *know*," Maddie said. "That's why going footwise on the stairs would take too long."

"You jumped here all the way from your window, didn't you?" Raven asked.

"I did, indeed," Maddie said, beaming. "Couldn't really see where I was going, though, so that's why I splanched the chair."

"I'm sorry to have to tell you this, Maddie," Raven said, "because I know you can do impossible things when you don't know they're impossible yet, but that kind of jumping definitely is. Impossible. Apple and I would 'splanch' and 'sminter' just like the chair."

"Toad droppings," said Maddie. "Last time I do that, then. And it was so fun, too."

Apple's stomach grumbled.

"Aaaah!" Maddie yelled, hopping away from Apple.

Apple laughed. "I'm just hungry," she said.

"I know! That's why I shrieked, because, oddness

gracious, to go so long without food that your stomach yells at you! What, did you think I thought you had a monster in your tummy? Don't be silly." Maddie leaned over to Raven and loudly whispered, "*Does* she have a monster in her tummy?"

"No." Raven laughed.

"Then let's take care of our poor, starving Apple," Maddie said, grabbing each girl by the hand.

The three girls trundled out the door and down the stairs. The windows poured light as thick and yellow as fresh butter on the stones, yet Apple couldn't feel anything but dread. What was wrong with her?

As they approached the Castleteria, the doors flung open. One of Sparrow Hood's Merry Men, hair thick with porridge, ran past.

"New hair treatment, Tucker?" Maddie asked, and got only grumbling in return.

"Hm. What do you think that was about?" Apple asked.

"It might actually have been a hair treatment," Raven said. "Tucker is terrified of turning bald like his dad."

They entered the Castleteria and saw how the Merry Man got his hair treatment.

The room was divided into two sides, the tension as thick as witch fog. On one side were the Royals—Apple's friends and others who wanted to keep their destiny. On the other side were the Rebels—Raven's friends and those who wanted to rewrite their destiny and make their own story, no matter who their parents were. Puddles of porridge lay splattered on the floor.

Apple marched into the fray. "What's going on?" she asked, and was answered by shouts from both sides.

"One at a time, please," Apple said. "Cedar?"

Cedar Wood stood between the two sides, a salad of leafy greens and acorns on her tray. Her dark kinky hair and her embroidered jumper dress were untouched by porridge, but her carved wooden face scrunched up as if wanting to cry.

"I don't know what to do," said Cedar. "Am I supposed to sit with my friends same as always? Or pick a side based on what I want? I'm not a Royal, but then again I *do* want my destiny, when I'll be changed from a puppet into a real girl, but then again, I *do* want others to be able to choose if they don't like their destiny so . . . so I don't know what to do now!"

"Briar, what happened?" Apple asked.

Briar Beauty popped her head up from behind the custard platter she was using as a shield. Her wavy brown hair and rose-pink minidress were also porridge-free.

"They threw food at us," she said. "So we retaliated. It was kind of hexciting!"

"They threw food first," Sparrow Hood called from the opposite side. His green fedora dripped porridge into the quiver of arrows on his back.

"*Liar!*" screamed Duchess Swan, her pale face turning red. The white feathers in her cap and her ballet-style skirt ruffled up as if they were as annoyed as she was. She picked up an entire bunch of bananas and cocked her arm back, ready to throw.

"Easy, Duchess," said Raven, stepping up beside Apple. On seeing Raven, a few of the Royals booed.

"You completely ruined our Legacy Day," said Daring Charming, standing with one leg propped up on a bench. His golden hair was as dazzling in the morning sunlight as his spotless white jacket.

"Not to mention our Legacy Day *dance*!" said Briar. "It was more like a funeral than a party. I worked really hard planning it."

"You did what you wanted without thinking of anyone else, didn't you, Raven Queen?" said Daring.

"Nothing was just right," Blondie Lockes said, shoulders slumped. A glob of porridge tangled in her fabulous golden ringlets. "Nothing at all."

"I...I thought Raven was very brave," said Cedar, taking a slow step toward the Rebels table.

"She doesn't want to be all evil-y—is that so wrong?" said Maddie.

"Definitely not," said Dexter Charming. He smiled at Raven. His brother Daring cleared his throat in warning, and Dexter looked down, adjusting his black-framed glasses. "I mean, this does pose some interesting philosophical questions. Raven's choice not only affected her own destiny but everyone's from the tale of Snow White, and so her actions keep expanding until—"

"We all have a destiny to fulfill," said Briar. "If I have to sleep for a hundred years as Sleeping Beauty, Raven should suck it up and take her turn being the Evil Queen."

"Yeah, look what happened when Raven's mother went off script!" said Hopper Croakington. His burgundy brocade jacket was smeared with porridge, though his freckled face and red hair remained clean. "She took over other fairytales and Wonderland, too, and was s-s-scary."

Hopper began to shiver with fright and then—*pop!*—turned into a frog.

"You're dangerous, Raven!" said Faybelle Thorn. She wore her cheerleading outfit, her midnight-blue hair in a high ponytail. "Stay the hex away from *my* fairytale—or else!"

"Oh, stop all this huffing and puffing," said Cerise Hood. She stood in the very back in the shadow of one of the Castleteria's great pillar trees, draped in her red hood and cloak as always.

"Who is going to make me?" asked Faybelle. "You?"

Cerise reached up, as if to make sure her hood was on straight, and backed away.

Cupid flew down on white feathery wings from where she'd been hiding in the branches of the tree. She ran a hand over her dusty-pink hair. "Raven just followed her heart. I'd advise everyone to do the same."

"Don't be naive," said Faybelle. "An Evil Queen who doesn't follow her destiny to the letter will cause a fairyload of damage. Her mom went rebel and stole the Sleeping Beauty villain role away from my mom. Now Raven thinks by rebelling she's avoiding becoming evil? Ha! More than ever, she's following in her mommy dearest's supremely evil footsteps. Raven Queen, if you refuse to follow your script, how can we trust anything you do?"

"I…I…" Raven stammered.

"Do what you're supposed to do," shouted Lizzie Hearts, waving her flamingo scepter. "And…off with your head!" she added as an ever-afterthought. Her gold crown and glossy black hair were untouched, but the red heart she always painted around one eye was smeared slightly as if she'd wiped porridge off her face.

"Friends," Apple said to the Royals side, opening her arms. "Please don't hexcite yourselves. We need to be *better* than this. We *are* better than this."

"Better than what?" Raven asked, approaching the Royals. Duchess adjusted her aim, pointing her bunch of bananas at Raven.

"She should stay over there," Duchess said. "On the other side, with the evil people."

Apple glided over, blocking the trajectory of the

bananas. "*Evil* is such a strong word, Duchess. Especially to use for everyone." She gestured at a table of Rebels, where Cedar cautiously set down her tray. "I mean, would anyone really call Maddie evil? Mad, yes—"

"Why, thank you. That's very kind," said Maddie, sitting cross-legged on the tabletop.

"—but, evil? No. And Hunter? Everyone loves Hunter Huntsman."

For some reason, Ashlynn Ella whimpered from the Royals table. She leaned over, her strawberry-blond hair hiding her face. Hunter stood up from his table. His hair was shaved on the sides of his head and the long part down the middle usually flopped over, but now, thick with porridge, it stood up like a Mohawk.

"Well, and what about Cerise?" Apple paused. It was hard to guess what was going on in that girl's head, always skulking around in the shadow of her red hood. "*Ahem*. Or…you know, Cedar? She's not evil. Why, she's the nicest puppet I've ever met."

"That's kind of an offensive term," muttered Nathan Nutcracker, sitting on the edge of a table swinging his little wooden legs.

"Sorry, Nate," Apple said. "I mean, the nicest *wooden person* I've ever met."

"Well, *she's* evil," piped up Blondie, pointing at Raven.

"And she's *supposed* to be evil," Apple said. "Or at least be working toward that end. It seems silly to get so upset at someone who just made a mistake. Royals aren't mean people, are we?"

Duchess lowered her bananas, and Briar shook her head.

"I think, in our hearts, we're not really mad at anyone," said Apple. "We're just worried about what we'll do now that Raven didn't sign the Storybook of Legends."

"Raven ruined Legacy Day for all of us!" Blondie yelled.

"She did not!" Cedar shouted back. "And I can't lie!"

"Raven made a mistake." Apple gestured to the Rebels side. "And they're her friends and naturally want to support her. But I believe that they will come around to embrace their destinies again."

"Wait," Raven said. "Is that what you think? That I was just impulsive? That I...I slipped and *accidentally* chose my own destiny and will go back on that choice any second now?"

"Of course!" Apple said, beaming. She faced the Rebels. "As president of the Royal Student Council, I mean, co-president..." She smiled at Maddie, who smiled back. She and Maddie had *both* been elected to the post, though that was taking some getting used to. Apple had always ruled alone. "I want you so-called Rebels to know you are still important to all of us here at Ever After High." She opened her arms as if to hug them. "Do you hear that, Rebels? We don't hate you! Not a bit! And we can be patient until you redecide to follow your destiny!"

"I'm *not* following my destiny," Raven said, folding her arms. "That's the whole point. You know it isn't fair to force me into being evil."

"But it's your destiny," said Apple.

"It should be my *choice*," said Raven.

Grumbles from both sides began to escalate into shouts.

Something was not right here. Apple was being reasonable. She was exuding kindness and sunshine, and yet the room seemed tenser and angrier than before she'd arrived. She didn't want the Royals going all big bad on the Rebels, but, of course, the Rebels were making dangerous choices they would simply have to undo or everything good and magical and hopeful in Ever After—all stories and destinies, all magic kisses and Happily Ever Afters—would unravel and disappear!

"No, listen!" Apple tried again. "I personally still value you even when you make huge mistakes—"

A spoonful of porridge flipped from Sparrow Hood's direction and landed with a *splat* on Apple's cheek.

Apple gasped. A stunned silence gripped the Castleteria.

Briar stood, pushing up her sleeves. "It's about to get all nonfiction in here."

"Bring it," said Cerise.

And then the real food fight began. Not just a few bowls of porridge this time. A megaeruption of an all-you-can-eat airborne buffet.

"Woo-hoo!" Maddie yelled, picking up a blackbird pie. "Now, this is a party!"

Duchess's banana bunch slammed into Cedar. Cerise Hood opened up with a barrage of cream puffs faster than Apple could follow.

Faybelle began to lead a cheer, her words creating a spell that sent food flying from her tray: "One, two, I'm glad I'm not you. Three, four, your aim is poor. Five, six—"

Someone chucked an entire peck of pickled peppers at her head.

Projectile hot cross buns flew past airborne pat-a-cakes, slamming into Rebels and Royals alike. Maddie stood on the table, laughing. An easy target, she was instantly covered in dripping eggs and gooey bean curd.

"How did...what *happened*?" Apple said, too stunned to move.

"Maybe it's us," said Raven. "Maybe it's our fault."

Apple nodded. Before they'd arrived, it'd been a little tense and a bit porridge-y. But Apple and Raven's presence seemed to have thrown a lit match into a haystack.

"We've got to—" Raven started, but was interrupted by a large glob of custard striking her in the face.

"The pot!" Apple said.

In the middle of the food fight, the monstrous pot of nine-day-old peas porridge was left untouched, as it always was. "Nine-day" was understood to be a polite understatement. Apple pulled Raven behind it, and they huddled there, covered in mess. Or rather, Raven was covered in so much mulberry custard and pumpkin pudding that she resembled a marsh goblin. Apple only had the smudge of porridge on her cheek. A robin passed by, wiped it off with a wing, and flew away.

"This has gotten royally out of hand," Raven said, digging some curds and whey out of her ear.

"I agree," Apple said. "Go talk to them."

"Me!?" Raven sputtered. "I'm not their leader."

"Well, the Rebels think you are, after your Legacy Day stunt and all. They're probably just waiting for you to take control."

"I don't want control. I just didn't want to be evil. They should do whatever they want. Besides, you're the co-president of the Royal Student Council! You fix it!"

Apple ducked lower as a rogue pat-a-cake flew over the pot. "I tried. And got a porridge pie in the face."

"That was you *trying*?" Raven asked. "The whole 'we love you even though you're stupid' bit?"

"Well, I didn't say 'stupid,' did I? That would have been rude."

"Telling people that you don't hate them is rude."

"What? And telling them I do hate them would be polite? That's just ridiculous!"

"No! It's…you don't understand," said Raven.

"I'm really trying to understand, Raven," said Apple. "But it's hard to stay cheerful and positive when I see people destroying destinies and causing Happily Never Afters."

"But…I didn't…*UGH!*"

Raven dropped her head into her hands and slumped against the pea pot.

"Ouch, hot." Raven scooted away.

Some liked it hot, Apple had heard. Some even liked it cold, though she had never met anyone personally. But what baffled her was that some actually liked it in the pot nine days old.

Peas porridge aside, everything seemed to be broken and backward. When there was a problem, Apple spoke, people listened, and it was fixed. Maybe what Raven had done on Legacy Day had broken more than just their story. What if it had broken Apple? What if who she was and everything she could do were just . . . gone?

She peered over the pot. Hunter Huntsman had always sat with the Royals. After all, he played a part in the Snow White tale and roomed with Dexter Charming. But today he was sitting with the Rebels.

"Destiny is a prison!" he shouted, and threw a soy turkey sausage patty into the fray.

The patty struck Ashlynn Ella dead in the face. She looked up at him, tears trembling in her eyes as the patty slowly slid down her cheek. Hunter stepped back, his eyes wide with horror.

"Ash, I'm sorry, I didn't mean—"

Her bottom lip trembled, and Ashlynn ran off, breaking into sobs. Hunter raced after her, as a personal-sized fairyberry pie smacked him in the back of his head. The sound of Ashlynn's wails mixed with Hunter's pleas broke Apple's heart.

Suddenly Maddie appeared around the pot, cherries peppered in her mint-and-lavender curls.

"Why are you guys hiding?" she asked. "Come join the fun!"

"It's not fun," Raven said. "They're angry and we don't know what to do."

"Don't be silly," said Maddie. "We used to have food fights in Wonderland regularly. Why, if a dinner party didn't end with a food fight, the host might be downright insulted. Not a single food fight has occurred since I came to Ever After, and I was beginning to think no one had any manners. Wait for me!" she yelled, running back into the middle of it and getting splattered by a chunk of grits.

Maddie squealed with delight, but other voices yelled, raged, wailed, and even wept.

Apple felt an unfamiliar scowl on her face. This *was* her fault. She'd promised Headmaster Grimm she would persuade Raven to sign. But Apple had failed and let the entire school down.

As the future Snow White, one day Apple would be queen of her mother's kingdom—that is, *if* she became Snow White. Apple knew she had to find a way to unite the school again and prove to herself she had what it took to be a great ruler. She stood up. It didn't matter that she might be pelted with porridge or mashed with potatoes. Sometimes doing the right thing was hard...and potentially messy. But a good leader always did the right thing.

Apple stepped out from behind the pot. But just then, the Castleteria went eerily quiet.

Masses of porridge, curds and whey, pies, and meats of various sorts were floating, motionless, each food missile halted midway between hurler and target. Both sides, Royals and Rebels, stared with wonder and fear. The food in the air pulled itself into a floating sphere.

The food splatter on Raven unpeeled from her skin and unwound from her hair, flying off like metal filings toward a magnet. All the food in the room crept, slid, and floated into the sphere and then slopped to the floor in a heap.

"What is going on?" Blondie said. "Raven, are you doing that? It looks like evil doings."

"It is," whispered Baba Yaga, who was suddenly standing next to Blondie.

Blondie screamed. The school's head of dark sorcery was short, her clothing ragged, her long gray hair snarled and stuck with tiny braids and bird bones.

"The food hurling is over," Baba Yaga stated, and then screeched "*Detention!*" and slammed her staff onto the ground. There was a flash, or rather, the opposite of a flash, a dark burping wave. Baba Yaga was gone, and the food was crawling onto itself and splitting into three large blobs standing on chicken-like legs.

"Food golems!" shrieked Gretel's son, Gus, who had an expression on his face that kept switching between fear and joy.

"*Jah*, you are right, Gus," said Hansel's daughter, Helga. "Food golems. But do vee eat dem or run from dem?"

The food golems began to strut forward.

"Uh...I vote run," said Briar.

But the food chickens herded the children, nudging them out of the Castleteria.

"But...but I'm Apple White," Apple said, her voice quavering. "I should avoid detention at all costs. What will my mother think?"

The golems didn't listen. And though starlings came to her rescue, attacking the golems and pecking at their cherry-tomato eyes and granola wings, the golems herded Apple toward the General Villainy classroom, same as everyone else.

A chill breeze whistled, raising mother-goose-bumps on Apple's arms. Portraits of famous villains leered at her from the walls—pirate kings, bad fairies, dragons, ogres, and the Marsh King. The chairs were black and rigid with spikes. A skeleton dangled from a display hook in the corner. It raised a bony hand to wave.

Apple sat at a desk and put her head on her arm. She seemed to have a hole inside her where the promise of her destiny used to beat like a heart.

CHAPTER 2

IN THE SERVICE OF DESTINY

RAVEN LAID HER HEAD ON THE DESK AND tried to ignore the hole inside her gaping with the uncertain future. But detention was quiet and boring, and Raven had nothing to do but think.

For as long as she could remember, she feared and fought against her destiny. Now that she was free, what would she do next?

She'd made a choice, one that she'd intended to affect her alone. But that choice not to sign had been like a pebble thrown into a pond, and the water rippled outward to her friends. From what she'd just seen in the Castleteria, the ripples were forming a tsunami.

Guilt settled into her empty stomach, where breakfast should have gone. She felt a little sick and close to tears. How had everything come undone? All this business with Legacy Day had stripped her down, made her feel raw and lonely and like a lost little kid separated from her mom at a busy market.

She glanced at her MirrorPhone and wished she could just call up her mother, say hi, know that she had someone out there who loved her no matter what. Her mother was not the lovey, cuddly, hot-chocolate-with-marshmallows type, but she did always have solid advice. She could call her kind father, but he might not have advice for her current situation. After all, he'd married her mother, a woman he knew he'd never be happy with, because it was in the script.

When she was six and asked her mother what to do about the kids who'd taped KICK ME, I'M EVIL signs to her back, her mother responded, "Kick them back. Turn them into bedbugs. Or ignore them, and they'll go away eventually."

Raven chose option three.

PROFESSOR MOMMA BEAR APPEARED AT THE General Villainy classroom door, an eight-foot brown bear in a frilly cap and apron. She smiled, which Raven always found a little alarming—so many sharp teeth beneath those kind brown eyes.

"Detention is over, my dears," Momma Bear said. "Headmaster Grimm would like all students in the Charmitorium immediately."

"Curses," Cerise muttered. "I was hoping we'd get some breakfast after all."

"If you're hungry, I could scrape some more curds and whey out of my ears," said Raven.

Cerise smiled and seemed about to banter back, but then she shrugged deeper into her hood and turned away.

Raven was about to go after her when Apple stepped up beside her. Smiling big.

"Don't ask, Apple," Raven said.

"Please poison me with a cursed apple?" she said.

"Apple…"

"Please, please, please be royally evil and try to

poison me so our story will happen? Pretty please? Charming please? Enchanting please?"

Raven sighed and started toward the Charmitorium. "Apple, I'm so sorry. I'm royally, rebelliously, forever-after sorry. I didn't mean to hurt you. But I *can't* be evil. And even though I didn't sign, I didn't go *poof* and disappear, like Headmaster Grimm threatened I would. So that means I have a choice about who I'll be, and I'm going to take it."

"You didn't go *poof* yet," said Apple, following after her. "Who knows how these things work? Maybe on Graduation Day, you'll just vanish in a puff of smoke? Before that can happen, I have to fix everything and make it all fair again, and setting you on the right path is the only way I can see."

"I think I'm already on the right path," said Raven. "I bet everyone will calm down in a couple of days and things will go back to normal. Well, mostly normal."

The massive Charmitorium held hundreds of seats facing the gilded stage. But since the whole school wasn't gathering today—just the second-year students who had been part of the food fight—

Professor Momma Bear directed them down to the seats in front.

The headmaster, Milton Grimm, stood on the stage before blue velvet curtains as the students shuffled in, his arms folded. He had black hair that was gray at his temples, a small mustache curled at the ends, and a gaze that made Raven wither.

Don't look at me, don't look at me, she thought, sinking deeper into her chair.

He looked at her.

Raven was used to the headmaster's disapproval, but today his eyes were so furious she almost felt the heat of his gaze clawing at her like dragon flame. Raven had been so hocus focused on deciding whether to sign the Storybook of Legends that she hadn't thought through some of the consequences. Ever After High's purpose was to prepare the children of fairytales to fulfill their destiny. A destiny Raven had rejected. Would Headmaster Grimm allow her to stay? Would she be sent home, away from Maddie and her friends, and break her kind father's heart?

"I am *vastly* disappointed," the headmaster said, "in all of you."

Beside Raven, Apple gasped, heartbroken.

"After yesterday's tragedy," the headmaster said, still glaring at Raven, "I expected somber students, ashamed of their involvement in ruining Legacy Day, repentant and eager to resume their studies. I certainly didn't expect a rebellious riot in the Castleteria! But I suppose that's the sort of chaos that comes when someone goes off script."

Raven felt every person in the Charmitorium turn to look at her. She slipped her hair from behind her ear and let it fall over half her face. Was now the part when he would expel her?

"Legacy Day is not only canceled, it's postponed indefinitely. I will not hold it again until you all show me you are mature enough to make wise choices. You know your roles. If we don't follow the rules, everything gets…messy. As you saw in the Castleteria today. *Ahem*."

He paused as if he had told a joke and was waiting for laughter. Two rows in front of Raven, Dexter Charming raised his hand.

"I'm not taking questions, Mr. Charming," Grimm said, and Dexter's hand dropped. "Despite what happened, your stories must go on. This school must go on. For the sake of our stories, our destinies, and the very existence of Ever After! You all need a reminder of just how important your roles are, and, therefore, I am moving up our annual Yester Day activities. Now, before you protest, changing the day of an activity does not count as breaking the rules."

"I don't think anyone thought that," Briar whispered to Apple. "Did you think that?"

"He's *disappointed* in me, Briar," Apple whispered back. "Surely he's thinking that I failed him and all of Ever After. And I did! I feel worm-riddled and rotten to my core."

Grimm was pacing the stage as if he was giving a performance or, perhaps, showing off his perfectly tailored three-piece suit.

"I'm not above *bending* the rules, of course," he said. "But only in the service of destiny. Everything we do is to keep those Happily Ever Afters coming. Yester Day is an important part of your journey to Happily Ever After, connecting you with a grand heritage of stories beyond your own and strengthening a community dedicated to the success of all destinies. As you celebrate Yester Day by meeting with exemplary fairytale characters of the previous generation, may you be inspired to follow your own destiny." He looked pointedly at Raven and cleared his throat.

So she wasn't getting expelled? Raven looked over at Maddie and smiled. Maddie took off her teacup hat and toasted her with it.

"Morning classes are suspended to give you time to download the Yester Day app on your MirrorPhone, browse its list of approved fairytale characters, select a few, and schedule visits."

The students busied themselves with their phones.

"Hey, Apple," said Humphrey Dumpty, leaning in from the row behind. He was so pale he made Apple White look tan. "I, um, I just took care of the install for you."

Apple's MirrorPhone beeped. She smiled. "So you did! How ever did you manage to do that?"

The smooth white cheeks of Humpty Dumpty's son began to color. "Well, um... you can push stuff, like apps and things, to another phone. If you, uh, have the person's password."

Raven perked up. "Humphrey has your password?"

Apple shrugged. "I gave it to him when we were working on something together. He only has my best interests at heart, isn't that right, MC Dump-T?"

Humphrey blushed so hard he appeared to be dyed pink. He cleared his throat. "True dat," he said, and he swaggered away, his squat body swaying with each step of his long, thin legs. Everyone nearby watched him go, tensing for Humpty Dumpty's son to trip and fall and for the inevitable sound of breaking. There was an audible sigh of relief when he made it out the door in one piece.

Raven tapped at her own phone. "Your password is *fairest*, isn't it?" she said, not looking up.

Apple gasped. "How did you know? Did you hack me?"

"Just a guess," said Raven. "You should probably change it to something a little less guessable. I know you're not worried about people breaking rules, but sometimes they do. You know. Speaking from experience."

"Okay," Apple said, tapping on her phone. "This should be more secure."

She showed Raven her screen.

NEW PASSWORD: -ZZ--ZZ--ZZ--Z-ZZ-Z--Z-ZZZ--Z-- ZZ--Z-Z-ZZZ--ZZ-ZZZ-Z--

"Overkill?" said Raven. "There's no way you'll be able to remember that."

"Sure I can. It's still *fairest*, but I converted it to Lulla-binary notation."

"Lulla-what?"

Apple shrugged. "My elective this year is Experimental Fairy Math."

Raven nodded slowly. It was easy to discount the Fairest One of All as nothing more than a lot of golden curls and cheery fashion choices. Raven reminded herself that Apple was fairy, fairy smart.

So how could a girl be so epically intelligent and yet not be able to see what Raven knew to be true? That destiny was just a lot of puppet strings, and happiness could only come with freedom?

Raven wasn't keen to stay under Grimm's scorching gaze, so she and Maddie ran down to the invisible grove on the croquet lawn to work on the app. Croquet games at Ever After High were rare, mostly because of that grove of invisible trees in the middle of the field. But they sprouted up one day and couldn't be chopped down until someone found an invisible ax. Croquet was a beloved sport in Wonderland,

and some believed that was why a Wonderlandish invisible grove had appeared there—or rather, not appeared, as it were.

Raven walked with her hands out, feeling for a tree, then sat down against it and scrolled through the characters available for visits. She checked under the *Q*'s for *Queen* and the *E*'s for *Evil*, but, of course, her mother had not made the headmaster's approved list. There was an "Evil Wizard Tim" and an "Evil Fairy Megan," but mentor options for those destined for evilness were sparse. Just as Headmaster Grimm had said in the assembly, everything was designed "to keep those Happily Ever Afters coming." And Happily Ever After meant the bad guy loses. Or dies. Or is locked up in a mirror prison forever after where her daughter can never visit.

There were lots of queens, though. Apple's mom, Ashlynn's mom, Briar's mom, Daring's mom. Every-body-who-wanted-Raven-to-be-evil's mom.

"Curses!" Raven shut the phone down. She wanted to talk to someone who had been a rebel and yet made it work. Or just someone who did something *different*, for fairy's sake! Raven needed a cauldron-load of advice. She'd only meant to make her own choice, not cause all this chaos and uncertainty. But in the few hours since Legacy Day, she'd been accosted constantly for guidance. First Ashlynn Ella, with teary eyes, pulled Raven into a broom closet and confessed her impossible love for Hunter Huntsman.

"I want to be with him forever after, but he isn't a prince, and I already signed the Storybook of Legends swearing to become the next Cinderella. What do I do?"

Later, Hunter had whispered to Raven the same secret question.

Cerise Hood had lurked nearby, her face full of questions she seemed afraid to ask. Cedar Wood had been distraught with the groupings of either Royals or Rebels, unsure where she fit. Even Sparrow Hood had asked if she had tips on getting all his Merry Men "on the same page."

"I don't know what you should do," Raven had told each of them individually. "Whatever feels right to you. It'll all work out."

And then the food fight. Raven squirmed with guilt. If she'd been an actual leader to the Rebels instead of a bewildered girl adrift in the aftermath of her own scary choice, maybe she could have done something. Calmed everyone down. Helped make a plan for what the next chapter might bring now that anyone could write a new destiny without fear of going *poof.*

"Maddie, where are you going for Yester Day?" Raven asked.

"I wanted to go to Wonderland, of course," Maddie said, hanging upside down from what appeared to be thin air. She reached out and plucked an invisible apple. "I'm keen to see the scenes that I haven't seen in umpteen weeks. Except in my dreams, of course. But I can't. Not for real and true."

Raven nodded. During her mother's attempt to take over Wonderland, the entire realm had been poisoned with a toxic madness that threatened to infect all of Ever After. The headmaster, Baba Yaga, and other magic folk had had no choice but to seal the portals to Wonderland to stop the infection from spreading. Maddie and her father, Lizzie Hearts, Kitty Cheshire, the White Queen, and a scant few others had managed to escape before the gates were sealed. Maddie didn't blame Raven for her mother's corruption of Wonderland's magical madness and ruining her homeland, but, still, every time Raven thought of the lost Wonderland, she felt awful, as if she'd been baked in a pie with four and twenty blackbirds.

"You're a gloomy Gus today." Maddie, still upside down, grabbed Raven by the shoulders and shook her. "Retreat, Gus! Back! Back! We wish to speak to Raven now!"

A small voice called from across the field. "I am no-vhere near you!" shouted Gus Crumb, who was scampering behind Cerise, along with his cousin Helga.

Raven laughed. "It's okay, Maddie. I'm just not sure who to visit for Yester Day."

"Oh. Right! The voice said you needed to find someone who was bad and made it good. Or was it the other way? No, that was it. 'Someone who had been a rebel and yet made it work,' right?"

"The voice?"

"You know, the Narrator. The one who describes what we're thinking or doing or whatever."

"Oh. You're still hearing that?"

"Sometimes. More often when I'm near you or Apple, for some reason." Maddie dropped down from the tree, landing on her hands, and did a somersault.

"Stop following me!" Cerise yelled at Gus and Helga, a covered basket hanging from her arm.

Gus rubbed his hands together. "But vhat does she haff in ze basket, my cousin Helga?"

"I do not know, my cousin Gus," Helga said. "But it ees smellink soooo delicious!"

"It's just food!" Cerise said. "*My* food! Go get your own!"

"She could share, maybe?" said Gus.

"*Ja*, she could share, no?" said Helga.

"*No*," said Cerise.

"Fine. She will enjoy ze delicious basket-food, und vee vill starve!"

Gus and Helga huffed back toward the school, and Cerise darted in the opposite direction, toward a cluster of trees.

"Poor thing," Maddie said.

Raven grunted. "I don't think they're going to starve."

"No, you silly! I mean Cerise. She usually eats alone." Maddie tapped a finger on her chin. "Maybe it's because she doesn't have any tea. Dad always says it's the tea that makes the party. Maybe if we give her tea, the party will follow!"

"Maybe," said Raven. "But maybe she wants to be alone. We had a talk recently. She, uh, confided in me some things about her family. I kind of thought that meant we were friends, but now she's avoiding me."

Cerise looked up, as if aware she was being watched. Maddie waved. Cerise waved back, and then checked to make sure her hood hadn't fallen down. Red Riding Hood's daughter was never without her own short cloak and hood, always up over her head.

An idea sparked in Raven.

"Ooh, I love it when ideas spark in you!" Maddie yelled—completely inappropriately, in the Narrator's humble opinion, since she only knew about the sparking idea by eavesdropping on the Narrator.

"Oh, Narrator, you are so silly," said Maddie. "Anywhatzit, what's your idea, Raven?"

On her MirrorPhone, Raven scrolled through the Yester Day app to "Red Riding Hood" and checked the box, showing Maddie triumphantly. But just a moment later she was rewarded with a message.

SEE THE HEADMASTER FOR APPROVAL.

"Oh, no." Raven meant to slump back against

an invisible tree but missed it and fell on her back. "Maddie, did you get a message like this when you signed up for a visit?"

"I did not, my purplish friend. Hey, can I call you Crow?" asked Maddie. She tossed an invisible apple core and reached out to pluck a new fruit. "That's the same bird as a raven, isn't it?"

"Sure," said Raven, staring at her phone.

"Thanks, Crow," Maddie said. She took a thoughtful bite of her invisible apple. "But that sounds like a different person than you. Crow, I'm going to call you Raven again."

"Maddie," Raven whispered, "I think I'm about to get expelled."

Maddie choked on a transparent bite of fruit. "No! Raven, I would turn into a muffin without you—a sad, dry, bran-and-wheat-chaff muffin that no one wants to eat and just crumbles away on a plate!"

"Don't turn into a muffin," said Raven, laughing despite herself.

"Don't worry. I'll come with you," Maddie said, holding out her hand.

Raven felt as if she could face almost anything with

Maddie by her side—hungry monsters, dark curses, even Headmaster Grimm. But Mrs. Trollworth, the headmaster's secretary, made Maddie wait in the hall, and Raven had to enter alone.

Alone except for the many autographed photos of fairytale characters staring at her from the wall. FOR MILTON GRIMM, THANKS FOR HELPING ME FOLLOW MY DESTINY!, Cinderella had signed. THANKS, GRIMMY! I NEVER COULD HAVE DEFEATED THE GIANT WITHOUT YOUR GUIDANCE, Jack had written.

Raven sat in the student throne across from Grimm at his desk. He sat back in his plush throne.

"Um…" Raven said.

Headmaster Grimm glared, flicking open the lid of an inkwell with the tip of a quill, and then flicking it shut again, open and shut. *Click click click.*

"If you were anyone else," he said slowly, "you would already be gone—expelled, bags packed, dropped down a wishing well on your way back home, to never set foot in my school again."

Raven's heart sank to somewhere below her ribs.

"Do you know why I am making a special exception for you, Miss Queen?"

"Um, because I'm special?" Raven asked.

She meant it as a joke, but the headmaster's frown deepened.

"It's the Snow White fairytale that is special," he said. "And you must play your part. Stories do have a way of working themselves out, but you need to *let* them and not thwart them at every opportunity."

"Um," she said, afraid to say anything else and change his mind about the not-expelling-her thing.

"You are staying because I'm giving you another chance. You *will* change your mind—eventually. And when you do, this little rebellion you stirred up will be squashed before it blooms."

Raven gulped. A response was bubbling up in her, but she wisely swallowed it down.

"Nevertheless," he continued, "there must be some consequences. During Study Ball, you will scrub the garbage chutes and think about destiny."

"If I'm cleaning during Study Ball, when will I have time to do my thronework?"

"Perhaps, if I keep you suitably busy, you won't have time to rebel out of boredom! You are here to learn how to become a dark sorceress and follow in your mother's"—Grimm shuddered—"evil footsteps. Though, perhaps, not her *exact* epically evil footsteps.

Ahem. So tell me, why, exactly, do you want to see Red Riding Hood?"

Raven examined his face. Did he know what Cerise had recently confided in her? That Mr. Badwolf—the same Mr. Badwolf who was Ever After High's professor of General Villainy—was actually Cerise's dad? Red Riding Hood and Big Badwolf's falling in love and marrying secretly were *not* part of the story. They did something that was crazy off-script. Now Raven had to know—did it work out for them? What happened to those who rebelled against destiny? Did their choice to rebel hurt others, as her choice seemed to be hurting her friends? How could she protect them?

"Well, it's a great cautionary tale about, you know, veering off the path," Raven offered.

Grimm nodded slightly. She was on the right track to convincing him.

"If Red had done what her mother had wanted and followed the path, she would have never met the wolf," Raven said. *And never fallen in love*, she thought.

Headmaster Grimm smiled. "That isn't the way the story is supposed to go, but I do get your point. It might be nice to discuss the regrets one feels for poor choices. Very well. One condition, though," the head-master continued, holding up a finger. "I want you to visit someone evil as well."

"Well, good role models for evil are rare, so maybe...I could maybe talk to my mom," said Raven quietly. Part of her longed to see her mother again just to ask her if she'd done right. Another part was afraid but thought the talk would provide a timely reminder of why she would do *anything* to keep from becoming like her.

"Your *mother*?" the headmaster whispered. Only a handful of people in all of Ever After even knew that Raven's mother wasn't dead but imprisoned far away in a magic mirror. Headmaster Grimm had sworn Raven to secrecy.

"Yeah, well, I thought—"

"Miss Queen, I hope that you are kidding," he said. "Though I find it in very poor taste to kid about the Greatest Evil Ever After Has Ever Known."

"Of...of course," Raven said. "Sorry. That was silly to suggest." She'd hoped he'd allow an extra MirrorChat this year, since he wanted her so badly to grow into her mother's role, but she shouldn't have risked asking. She winced, afraid he'd bring up expulsion again.

"You will visit the Candy Witch," Milton Grimm said. "She is a villain who wholeheartedly embraces her role. Er, just try not to get near her oven."

"Right...okay," Raven said. Raven knew the Candy Witch's daughter, Ginger, from school but had heard alarming stories about Ginger's mother.

"Off with you!" Mr. Grimm puffed, making shooing motions with his hands.

Raven was eager to oblige.

When she emerged into the hall, Maddie was sitting on the floor.

"You're still waiting for me!" said Raven.

Maddie popped up and gave her a hug. "Sometimes after talking to the headmaster, you get trembly and chin-quivery and even gloomier-Gussy. So I thought, maybe my friend Raven will need a hug."

Raven hugged her back. "I think I did. Thanks."

Maddie pulled a pink top hat off her head, stuck her arm in up to the elbow, and pulled out a hot cup of tea. "Also this. Hugs and tea. Cures everything."

Raven sipped. The warm charm blossom tea felt

like drinking down a hug. Though it couldn't entirely fill that hole inside her, aching with fear and confusion. Her mother would understand how it felt to be booed when she walked into a room. Though instead of working to better understand and lead her peers, her mother's solution would likely involve magic potions and zapping.

Maddie stood back and squinted. "You don't *look* expelled."

"I'm not!" said Raven.

"Aha! The tea worked!"

The tower bell rang. Maddie ran off to Chemythstry class. Raven finished her tea on the way to her Tall Tales lecture, taking a seat beside Cerise Hood.

"Hey," Raven said. "You know what the lecture is about?"

Cerise said, "Sneaking, I think, or—"

"*Skulking!*" shouted Professor Jack B. Nimble, appearing at the lectern seemingly out of nowhere. Several of the teachers applauded.

There were lots of Jacks. Raven had a hard time keeping them all straight. The Sprat one was the easiest, because he was extraordinarily skinny.

"You probably didn't know," Jack shouted, "that I was here for a full! Five! Minutes! Before I spoke!"

Raven winced. The megaphone mounted to the podium magnified his yelling till her ears squeaked, killing any hopes of a whispered conversation with Cerise. Raven slumped in her chair and pulled out her MirrorPhone.

"Misdirection!" he said, shouting now. "Magic for the nonmagical!"

Raven found Cerise's number and sent her a hext.

RAVEN: Hey C! loud, right?

There was a subtle buzz. Cerise checked her phone and then looked at Raven, eyebrow raised.

RAVEN: I know. using MirrorPhone in class = bad, but I have spella good news!

"*Behold!*" Jack shouted from the stage. He was holding an egg.

"That's my egg!" someone shouted from the audience. Several people gasped.

CERISE: Is news that Jack is done talking? ;)
RAVEN: HA! No. I get to visit ur mom for YD!

"Ah!" Jack shouted. "But did I take the egg five minutes ago, or just now? *You don't know!*"

Raven noticed something in Cerise had slumped.

CERISE: cool
RAVEN: Like u to come with me if u can
CERISE: ?
RAVEN: Luv to talk to ur M about going off book, but not sure she'd trust me with her secret. Unless u come?

"But the *skulk*," Jack continued. "The *skulk* is about the shrouding of the self without sacrificing movement. Watch!"

More people gasped, and Raven looked up at the stage again. Jack was gone.

"You aren't being very sneaky," someone whispered in her ear. Raven turned, and no one was there.

"Am I here?" Jack shouted from somewhere far behind Raven. Everyone looked and saw nothing.

"If anyone looks this way, they're going to see

you using your MirrorPhone," whispered someone behind her. She whirled to see, again, nothing. Curses, but he was good!

"*Here I am!*" Jack shouted, suddenly popping up in front of Raven. Raven shrieked, and everyone laughed or clapped. Jack smiled and looked around at everyone except Raven, but somehow was still whispering right at her. "Stay unnoticed by looking somewhere else. Show focus on everything but what you're actually doing." He walked away, waving at everyone, his voice receding. "And maybe learn to type blindfolded...."

"I'll go with you," Cerise whispered in her ear, and Raven jumped, off-balance from all the surprise whispering. "Sorry," Cerise said, slinking back into her seat, and her cloak.

"No, don't be," Raven said. "Thank you! We're going to have an amazing time tomorrow."

Cerise smiled, and the teeth that peeked out made Raven wonder how people hadn't realized that Mr. Badwolf was her father a long time ago.

CHAPTER 3

MADDIE CHATS WITH THE NARRATOR

Unwilling

Hey, Narrator!

Yes, Maddie?

Oh, hi! I was just wondering, why are you more talkative when I'm around Apple or Raven?

Well, they're the point-of-view characters for this particular story. Narrators like to follow the characters who do the most stuff, and in the story I'm currently telling, that's Apple and Raven. It's a fascinating philosophy really, you see—

Fascinating, yeah. So where are you going for Yester Day?

Oh! You're thoughtful to ask. But it's just for students, and I graduated long, long ago and far, far away, so to speak. I'll just observe what you all do. My daughter, though—

Wait, you have a daughter?

Um…never mind, I'm not supposed to get personal. So what are your Yester Day plans?

Since I can't go to Wonderland, I thought about visiting some of the people in Neverland. You know, because it's a relative of Wonderland. They both have the same last name: Land. Maybe they're even sisters. Sisters are often similar, right?

I can't advise you, Maddie. You know I am just supposed to observe the story.

Oh, I know, and you do a really good job of it.

Why, thank you.

Though you are so secretive sometimes I just want to blow out my cheeks and call myself a balloon! I mean, you knew all along that Mr. Badwolf was Cerise's dad, didn't you?

Uh…

So it's true!

But…but I didn't confirm anything!

Or deny, either. Oh, I just love our little talks. Thanks, Narrator!

Argh!

CHAPTER 4

JUST BE

~~HAPPY~~ Merry

OLD KING COLE WAS EVERY BIT THE MERRY old soul Apple was expecting. Even beneath a thick white beard longer than he was tall, you could tell he was constantly smiling. He was roundheaded, round-bellied, everything about him a bouncy ball of merriness.

"*Sit! Eat! Play checkers!*" he said when she arrived, his normal speaking tone a cheery shout.

"Thank you," she said.

Apple settled into one of the low, cozy pillow chairs

in his royal receiving room and moved a red checker on the board. Even that made the king laugh.

Old King Cole had attended one of her mom's dinner parties once. While some of the royal guests sat stiffly at their dinners with raised pinkies and bored eyes, Old King Cole had laughed. He laughed when the servants brought out the bread course, he laughed when he spilled his soup, he laughed and laughed till everyone else was laughing, too.

Apple figured that a man that happy must hold the secret to successfully ruling a kingdom.

"I was hoping you could tell me, Your Majesty," she said, "how a ruler might manage public unrest."

"Eh?" he said, holding a hearing trumpet up to his ear.

She leaned forward and politely spoke into it.

"How do you manage unrest?"

He played two quick jumps on the checkerboard. *"Drink some warm milk, dearie! Ha! Or check for peas under your mattress!"*

"No, not lack of rest." She jumped a checkers piece over one of his. "I mean, more specifically, how should a monarch handle ill will in the populace?"

"William Poplas is ill again? We used to call him Illy Willy in nursery-rhyme school! Ha!"

"Yes," she said, smiling, not sure if he was telling a joke. "Well, do you have any experience in dealing with angry mobs?"

"Is 'angry mobs' the name of one of those roc *music bands? Ha! The ones that sound like a giant bird shrieking?"*

"I, um…" Apple was doing her best to follow this conversation. A roc was a monstrous bird of legend.

"You can keep your hipping and hopping and knuckle-rapping music! I'll stick with my fiddlers three!" The king gestured to the two old women with violins in the corner who were playing the same jaunty tune over and over.

Apple frowned. "There are only—" she started, but the two violinists widened their eyes and shook their heads earnestly. Apple shut her mouth.

"I'm just teasing you, my girl!" said the king. *"Listen, the populace is happy when their ruler is happy. So just be merry!"*

Old King Cole slapped one of his checkers forward. *"King me! Ha! Or don't bother! I'm already king! Ha ha!"*

Perhaps Old King Cole hadn't been the best choice. He *was* a merry old soul. But Apple was certain that laughing loudly couldn't solve Ever After High's problems.

She let him beat her at checkers before taking her leave and skipping out to the Cole Castle wishing well. She opened her MirrorPhone, selected another character's location on her Yester Day app, and stood on the well's edge.

The water blinked silver below her, and Apple swallowed. No matter that it was 100 percent safe, traveling by wishing well gave Apple witchy chills.

She sang a couple of nursery rhymes to calm her pounding heart, pushed SUBMIT on her phone, and jumped in.

She heard a splash but felt no wetness, only a cool whoosh like a sudden spring wind. Through her tightly shut eyes, she could see flashes of light. Her stomach felt full of winged pixies, and when she peeked, she was inside a glowing sphere, rising above the water of a different well. She pressed END on her MirrorPhone. The sphere bounced her up and out, and as soon as her feet touched down on the grass beside the well, the sphere popped like a soap bubble.

Apple brushed off her spotless red-and-gold

skirt, fluffed the puffed sleeves of her quilted white jacket, and took in her surroundings.

The wishing well stood near the Buff Castle drawbridge. The castle itself was built of pale wood rising to square towers. *Emperor and Empress Buff.* They might be helpful. After all, they'd had to deal with some uncomfortable issues with that whole invisible-clothing fiasco.

The grand front doors opened to a servant in a red jacket adorned with several hundred brass buttons.

"Princess Apple," he said, bowing deeply. "We have been expecting you."

A warm, fruity draft came rolling out the door.

"Mmm," she said. "Apples."

The servant beamed. "In honor of your visit, the pastry chef is making apple tarts!" He paused. "Though, er, now that I think about it, perhaps that was rude. It's not as if we're implying a desire to bake you into a pie...."

Apple laughed. "It didn't even cross my mind," she said, though it had. "I think I would love apple desserts even if my name were something silly, like Pear."

He stared, his mouth a little open.

"Did I say something wrong?" she asked.

"*My* name is Pear," he whispered.

"Oh," she said. "I'm sorry. What a lovely name."

He coughed, cleared his throat, and seemed to remember himself. "Please come in."

As they entered the grand hall, Apple heard shouting.

"Jason! Put that on this instant! Our guest will be here any minute!"

Apple smiled, assuming the empress was dressing her young son. But when Apple entered the receiving room, there was no child to be seen.

The empress was tall, imposing, and beautiful, and she wore as many layers of clothing as seemed to be physically possible—silk camisoles, ruffled cardigans, fur-lined capes, skirts with a dozen petticoats, and a huge belt over it all. She was so stiff with clothes she could barely bend her arms. Perhaps, Apple considered, the empress was overdressed in contrast to the man beside her, who wore nothing but loose cotton shorts and a leather vest. Apple realized it was the emperor himself the empress had been hastily dressing. She supposed that old habits die hard.

"Emperor and Empress Buff, may I present Princess Apple White," Pear announced, bowing.

The emperor was lounging on a beanbag, his bare feet resting on a side table. He was stout, bald, and clean-shaven.

"What up, Apple!" said the emperor, lifting two fingers in the peace sign. The empress closed her eyes briefly and sighed.

"It is a pleasure to have you among us, Princess Apple, daughter of Snow White," the empress said. She dismissed the servant.

"Good-bye, Pear! It was nice to meet you!" Apple called after him.

The empress frowned. "Why did you just call my servant a fruit?"

"Oh, he told me that was his name."

"His name is Pear?" the emperor asked. "That's pretty cool."

They didn't know his name? Apple knew all one hundred and twenty-four workers in her castle by name.

"Your Majesties, thank you for seeing me. I've come with a lot of questions," said Apple. "I am co-president of the Royal Student Council—"

"Ah, I was president myself," said the empress.

"Wonderful!" Apple said. "I'm in a situation that I've never encountered before."

Apple told the empress about Raven, Legacy Day, and the food fight. The empress's eyes widened, her jaw clenched, her lips pursed together harder and harder.

The empress stood in a flourish of petticoats and capes. "By all that is golden, girl, how could you let it get to this point?"

"I, well, I ... it ..." Apple stammered.

"Order is the cornerstone of authority," the empress said, raising her arms up as if to catch and hold the entire world. She looked at Apple with piercing green eyes and put a heavy hand on her shoulder. "Once you lose control, you *cease* to be a leader."

Apple gulped.

Through an open window, Apple heard someone yelling far away. The queen turned her head, like a dog listening for prey. She smiled.

"Perfect. Come, take my hand. You will practice being a queen."

They marched out hand in hand, but Apple felt as if she were on a leash.

"I'll just stay here," the emperor called after them. "Maybe slip into something more comfortable."

The empress pulled Apple through several corridors and into an enormous pantry. In the courtyard beyond the kitchen door, several servants were trying to shush two yelling men.

"What are they arguing about?" Apple asked.

"It doesn't matter," the empress said. "If you appear to care, you risk getting dragged into their mess. Now, march out there and take control."

"But—" Apple started.

"Do it! Be the queen now that you will one day become. Show no weakness. Show no mercy. Make them do exactly as you say. You must master absolute control!"

The empress gave Apple a small push.

Apple walked forward, practicing angry faces and stomping her foot. She had to succeed. She had to. The happiness of all her friends at Ever After High was at stake.

"Stop it!" she yelled. "Now!"

The arguing did stop. Could it be this easy?

"That's Apple White," someone said. "Snow White's daughter."

"Yes," said Apple White. "Empress Buff sent me here to stop all this...this...arguing! At once!"

Pear turned to the two men, two farmers, each standing before his own wagonload of produce.

"You're lucky!" Pear whispered. "I was trying to warn you. You do *not* want the empress to hear any arguing. At least she sent this kind, generous princess in her place."

Apple flushed. Kind and generous princesses don't usually yell and stomp their feet. She cleared her throat. "So...whoever is making the ruckus had better just leave...now, um...if you'd be so kind."

One of the farmers bowed his head, his chin quivering. He was short with a nearly square face and large ears. "I just wanted a chance to sell my crop to the pretty castle."

"Oh, you've never sold here before?" Apple asked.

The farmer shook his head. "My wife's been sick, so I daren't leave her for as long as it takes to walk all the way to market. I was hoping—"

"Well, Buff Castle is *my* customer," said the other farmer. "You can't go stealing other farmers' customers!"

"Don't you shout at me!" shouted the first farmer, and it started all over again.

"Please," Apple tried to say. "Please, if you'd just...I have an idea if you'd calm—"

"*Enough!*" said the empress, appearing in the threshold. "You!" She pointed at the farmers. "Leave. Now. And you!" She turned her pointy finger on the servants. "Get back to work."

Everyone scurried away like blind mice faced with a carving knife.

"That, Apple White, is how you maintain control," said the empress with a pleasant smile.

The empress glided back into the castle. From down the corridor, Apple could hear her shout, "Jason! Vest on! *Now!*"

And Apple was left alone in the kitchen courtyard. She stomped her feet. She tried shouting, "Behave! Right now!" She imitated the empress's intimidating scowl.

"Apple?"

Apple whirled around. There stood Holly O'Hair. Her thick, long hair was done up in dozens of braids and hung in loops so it wouldn't drag on the ground. Apple scowled, feeling embarrassed, but Holly must have mistaken her expression for annoyance.

"Oh, I'm sorry, should I call you Miss White?" said Holly. "Or Your Majesty, or..."

"No, no, Holly, of course you can call me Apple."

"Oh, okay. It's still just so amazing to me that the actual daughter of Snow White is my actual friend! So what were you doing just now? Practicing a dance or something?"

"Um, well, er, hey, what are you doing here?" she deflected.

"Researching fashion," Holly said, gesturing. Across the courtyard stood a cottage, and through the window Apple could see mannequins and sewing machines and tailors busy at work. "I never thought about fashion when I was homeschooled, but so many people at Ever After High are interested in it, so I thought I'd add a fashion column to the school newspaper I'm starting. Since I already interviewed all the tower fairytale characters for Yester Day, I'm using the rest of my time talking to experts in fashionable and edgy clothing designs. I thought Emperor Buff's tailors would be good, since they made the most famous clothes in all of fairytales."

"Or they didn't…"

"Right." Holly pushed a stubborn lock of hair out of her face and took a step closer. "Hey, are you okay?"

The honesty of the question startled Apple. She

shrugged. "I . . . I'm not sure I know how to be a good queen."

Holly gasped and grabbed Apple's hands. "Apple, don't think that! You're perfect!"

"No," Apple said softly. "Empress Buff tried to show me how to lead through control and intimidation but . . . I failed. And I just felt so bad for those farmers. After all, Buff Castle must go through a great deal of produce." Apple started pacing. "Perhaps they could temporarily reduce the original order by twenty percent and purchase that amount from the new farmer, thereby allowing him enough steady income to risk staying home from the market and selling locally so he can be nearby while his wife is recovering. But maybe I'm wrong and a queen can't buy from both farmers, and a co-president of the Royal Student Council can't please both Royals and Rebels, and everything is . . . is a poisonous mess."

"Um . . . what?" said Holly.

"Never mind," said Apple. "See you back at school?"

Apple hurried away to the wishing well, feeling the entire weight of Ever After pressed down on her shoulders.

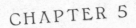

CHAPTER 5

TORCHES AND PITCHFORKS
and Other Hometown Traditions

THE MORNING WAS DIM, WOLF-GRAY CLOUDS pouncing on the sun. Raven tugged on a black wool sweater as she and Cerise waited in line for the school's wishing well. Holding her MirrorPhone inside her sleeve, she practiced hexting without looking.

Cerise looked at her phone and laughed. "Why did you just tell me 'Thus kind is slur'?"

"Oops. I meant to type 'This line is slow,'" said Raven.

She kept practicing while the line inched forward.

Ashlynn and Hunter were whispering behind her. Taking a cue from Jack, Raven listened without looking.

"Who are you visiting?" Hunter asked.

"Oh, you know, some princesses and queens," said Ashlynn.

"Right. So you can learn how to follow your destiny. And marry a handsome prince. And live in a castle. And be happy forever after."

"Hunter, stop, please. I don't know what else I can do."

Hunter's sigh was full of pain. "Neither do I."

Cerise was bouncing nervously on the balls of her feet. She leaned close to Raven and whispered, "My mom might be afraid to talk about...the *situation*. Such a marriage is forbidden in our village. Both sides would freak out if they knew."

"Both sides?"

"The Wolfs and the Hoods. You'll see."

Cerise pulled out her phone and selected Red Riding Hood from the Yester Day app. She leaped easily over the edge of the well and directly in, holding her hood on with one hand and winking at Raven as she dropped into the water.

Raven followed right after, the dry rush through water pushing her hair out of her face. She rose up and out of another well, landing on her feet.

Around her the Dark Forest was thick and sticky with evergreens. Sunlight sliced through the canopy in slim, cathedral-lighting shafts, lending just enough light for ferns and a few wildflowers to creep out of the dark soil. Ahead was a cottage, and beyond that, a village in a clearing.

"My parents built their house here so they'd be close to the wishing well," Cerise said as they walked to the cottage. "Dad can come for visits anytime, sneak in the back door, and no one sees."

"So who does everyone think your dad really is?" Raven asked.

"Oh, Hoods don't ask questions," Cerise said. "We're a very private people. I think most people assume the Huntsman was my dad. That would make more sense to them than the truth."

"But that would make you Hunter's sister!" said Raven. "Besides, you're not Cerise Huntsman—you're Cerise Hood. Hey, are you related to Robin and Sparrow Hood?"

"Distantly," said Cerise. "And let me emphasize—*distantly*."

The cottage was built of warm-colored wood, with green-painted windowsills and a thatch roof. Cerise opened the back door smoothly and silently, without a squeak in the hinges. They were kept well-oiled, Raven realized, for Cerise's dad's visits. Even the door hinges helped keep the Hood family secret.

Inside was a cozy family room, wooden furniture fit with comfy cushions. It would have been lovely, if Raven could have seen very well. But the windows were dark, with all the curtains closed, just low flames from a few fairy lamps to light the room. She peered at the framed photos on the walls. Every one was of Cerise: Baby Cerise, gnawing on a chew toy that looked remarkably like a bone; Toddler Cerise, chasing a chicken; Little Girl Cerise, climbing a high tree; Teenage Cerise, posing with her mother in front of Ever After High on the first day of school.

Nowhere in sight was a family photo of Cerise with both of her parents.

"Mom?" Cerise called out.

Red Riding Hood emerged from the kitchen wearing a floured apron. She was tall and lean, not as broad-shouldered as her daughter. She and Cerise shared the same straight dark brown hair, but Cerise's had a shock of white at the forehead, and Red didn't cover hers with a hood.

"Cerise!" Red ran forward and swept her daughter up in a hug. "You're here! I've missed you so much. And what perfect timing, because I just finished a batch of mini pecan pies."

"Mom has a business selling pastries," Cerise said to Raven.

"Oh, it's just a hobby, really," said Red.

"A hobby? She shipped twenty thousand fairyberry scones last year alone!"

Red laughed. "You're my biggest fan. Are you here for Yester Day? When I got the hext from Headmaster Grimm, I didn't imagine I'd be treated to a visit from my own daughter."

"Mom, this is my friend Raven. She wanted to meet with you especially. You see... she knows."

Red's eyes widened. "She knows?"

"She knows," said Cerise.

Red ran to lock the back door, checked the lock

on the front door, and then went from window to window, pulling the drapes shut even tighter.

"I knew this day would come, but I'm not ready."

"It's okay, really, Raven's great at keeping secrets."

"If they knew," Red was saying as she collapsed onto the couch, "if any of them knew, the Hoods or the Wolfs, Cerise would not be welcome home. The ignorant, stubborn fools."

"I don't understand," said Raven. "Cerise didn't do anything wrong."

"It doesn't matter," said Red. "Her father and I went off script. The story says that we're enemies. The Hood and Wolf clans remember that every hour of every day. How Baddy and I forgot long enough to fall in love..."

"Will you tell me the story?" Raven asked, sitting beside her. "I need to know if there's any hope when someone rebels against their destiny."

"Hope?" Red shook her head. "Listen, the very day after I graduated from Ever After High, I made my way to Grandma's house with my basket of treats, ready to face my destiny. Baddy—sorry, Badwolf—he approached me in the forest like he was supposed to, tried to get me to go off the path, you know, so he could get to Grandma's house first. Just like the story goes. Only, I realized I wasn't scared of him. He made me laugh!

"He started making up all kinds of excuses to make me leave the path." Red lowered her voice to imitate her husband. " 'There's, uh, a scorpion on the path up there, so you should probably go another way. Or it could have been a piece of wood that looked like a scorpion. Also, uh, the dirt on this path is enchanted, and when it gets wet it develops a ravenous hunger for boots. And slippers. Any footwear, really. So if you take the path, it will eat your shoes. And did I mention the scorpion?' "

"He's never been very subtle," Cerise said with a fond laugh.

"Baddy was in his human form, and, I admit, I thought him very handsome." Red blushed the color of her name. Raven raised her eyebrows in a question.

"The Wolfs *are* wolves," Cerise explained. "But many, like my dad, can transform between wolf and human form."

"Oh, okay. I wondered," said Raven.

"When I got to the cottage and Baddy was there in

my grandmother's hat and nightgown, pretending to be her..." Red snickered. "Can you imagine? And I was supposed to not notice it's him, but I was dying, and I could tell he was dying, too, both of us trying so hard not to laugh, because this was our destiny! This was the story we were born to tell, and how could we not take it seriously? Poor Grandma sat forever in the closet waiting to be rescued, but Baddy and I didn't want the moment to end, so we made up more and more things to say. 'My, what big, uh, nostrils you have.' 'All the better to sneeze with.' 'My, what big fingernails you have.' 'All the better to paint a lovely shade of red.' Eventually, he was supposed to attack me, and I could tell he didn't want to. So I ran and screamed, and he snarled, but neither of us could take it seriously until..."

Red paused, and her chin trembled.

"The Huntsman came," said Raven.

Red nodded. "With his ax. And he was supposed to kill Baddy, just kill him right there. But I... well, I'd learned a few things at Ever After High, and I, er, dropped a smoke bomb. And yelled '*Fire*.'"

"A smoke bomb?" Raven asked.

"I always carry a couple in my basket," Red said.

"Just for protection. Baba Yaga taught us how to make them."

"Was she all young then?" Raven asked, trying to imagine.

"Gracious, no," Red said. "She was ancient."

Raven tried picturing Baba Yaga as a baby—already wrinkled, gray-haired, and crabby.

"So, after that, the Huntsman left?" Raven asked.

"Yes, once he saw that Grandma and I were safe and that the wolf was nowhere to be seen."

"What happened after?"

"Well, we found ways to meet. Hoods aren't supposed to go into the forest. That's the Wolfs' domain. And Wolfs aren't supposed to get near the village. But Baddy and I would leave notes for each other in a hollow tree and meet far, far away from the village and the Wolf dens where no one could hear us, because as soon as we'd start talking, we'd start laughing, and Baddy has an outrageously loud laugh." Red blushed at the memory. "We got married in Wonderland, just the two of us, the Mad Hatter presiding. My bridesmaid was a rabbit in a bow tie, and Baddy's best man was a dormouse. It was all perfectly mad and just as crazy as our love. As happy as we were, I didn't feel really right away from home. Hood Hollow is my setting, after all. So for better or for worse, we returned home and have been living as a family in secret ever since."

Cerise sat beside her mother. Red took her daughter's hand and smiled sadly.

"Is it really so bad?" said Raven, attempting to cheer herself up as well as the Hoods. "After all, Beauty fell in love with the Beast."

"That was their *destiny*," said Red. "But even scripted love between a Hood and a Wolf would not go down well in Hood Hollow. The hatred between the clans is old, deep, and illogical, but very, very real."

"Was it worth it?" Raven asked.

"Of course," said Red. "I mean, we have Cerise. And each other. But . . . but it's hard, too. If our clans knew about Cerise, they'd consider her an abomination! I do sometimes wonder if we were selfish. Falling in love was our choice, but by going off script, we condemned our daughter to a life of secrecy."

"And I'm tired of the secret," said Cerise. "Maybe it's time to take off the hood."

"No," said Red quickly. "No, Cerise, you don't know how serious the consequences would be."

Cerise slumped back against the sofa, her whole face a frown.

"Your destiny wasn't fair," said Raven. "So you rebelled. I know that couldn't have been easy."

"I would do it again," said Red. "But you should know, being a rebel takes a lot more work than going along with the status quo. If you're thinking of trying to change your destiny, Raven, know that it will be much, much harder than you expect."

"Too late," Raven whispered.

"Mom, I don't know if Dad told you already, but Raven didn't sign the Storybook of Legends on Legacy Day," said Cerise.

"What? That was you?"

"She's...well, she's just the bravest person I've ever known. Besides you and Dad. If she can change her destiny, why can't—?"

A noise outside interrupted them.

"What now?" Red said.

She cracked open the door. The Hoods were gathering in the village center with torches and pitchforks.

Cerise rolled her eyes. "Every. Single. Time. Someone misplaces a shoe, and they go straight for the torches and pitchforks."

She moved past her mother to see what was going on, and Raven followed. A mob of Hoods had gathered by the stream that separated the village from the encroaching forest on the other side. A man in front was holding up a young wolf dressed as a sheep, gripping him by the back of his fluffy costume.

"Wolfs!" the man shouted toward the shadowy trees. "How dare you? We will not stand for this breach of rules!"

"It was just a dare!" the young Wolf howled.

Raven saw the shadows between the trees shift, and then a dozen wolves appeared, black and gray and brown, with yellow eyes and teeth exposed in snarls. The one in front stood on his hind legs and became a man with pointy ears, heavy beard, and some serious sideburns. He was also, magically, fully dressed.

"Let him go," the wolf-were said. "He's a child."

"Planting your spies in our herd, are you?" shouted a Hood.

"If we did, it'd be all the better to see you with," replied the Wolf with a snicker.

"Next you'll invade our homes, all the better to smell us."

"Don't worry, we can smell your stench miles away," another Wolf growled.

The two sides kept shouting at each other, and in the middle of it all, the young wolf shivered.

"Don't say anything about their teeth—that's when they attack."

"Stay away, grandma-eaters."

"You can't prove anything!"

If they'd been in the Castleteria, pickled peppers and peas porridge hot would have gone flying. *Do something*, Apple had pleaded with Raven then.

But I don't want to be a leader, Raven thought. *I don't know how to lead.*

The young wolf whimpered, sounding as afraid and alone as young Raven at nursery-rhyme school, the only future villain in the class, ignorant of the KICK ME, I'M EVIL sign taped to her back.

"Hey, stop it!" Raven yelled. She lifted her hands intending just to do a loud pop spell and get their attention, but it backfired. A burst of black air exploded, knocking both the Hoods and the Wolfs onto their rumps and singeing a few eyebrows. The wolf in sheep's clothing fell to the ground and scurried over the bridge to his clan. The Hoods barely noticed. They were all staring at Raven.

"It's...it's *her*...."

"The Evil Queen's daughter..."

"Get her."

"Get her!"

"*Get her!*"

The Hoods jumped to their feet and grabbed Raven, dozens of hands on her arms and legs. Raven couldn't even manage to squirm.

"No! Stop!" Cerise yelled.

"We don't allow witches in Hood Hollow," said a Hood man. "Let one witch in and next thing you know a whole crowd of gingerbread-housed, child-eating, cackling cauldron stirrers move in, taking up space and changing everyone into frogs."

"Or worse, into wolves!" a grandfather shouted.

"But that's not just any ordinary witch!"

"That's *her* daughter!"

"Get rid of her before she goes off script and destroys Hood Hollow like her mother destroyed Wonderland!"

"The only thing to do is dunk her."

"Yes, toss her in the river. She'll float downstream and become someone else's problem."

"Dunk the witch! Dunk the witch!" the mob began to chant.

"You can't," Cerise yelled. "Raven is good. She's helped me see I can write my own destiny!"

No one paid her any attention. Dozens of hands lifted Raven above the heads of the mob. They carried her onto the bridge.

"No!" said Cerise. "Not Raven. I won't allow it. I won't."

The mob kept chanting, holding Raven up. She could see the stream swirling below her. It looked cold. And a lot deeper than she was expecting. And were those wicked sharp rocks in the depths? Raven writhed, trying to fight her way free. This wasn't a joke. She was about to get seriously hurt. Or worse. She opened her mouth to mutter a spell, too scared now to worry about the spell backfiring. But someone shoved a sock in her mouth.

This is what she got for interfering. She wasn't a leader. She didn't know how to reason with people. She just needed to give up, improve her skulking skills, and hide her way through the rest of her time at school. Any time she attempted to help, it backfired, just like her magic.

"*No!*" Cerise yelled.

And then she howled. The sound froze Raven's blood and stopped the chant dead in the mob's throats.

Cerise's eyes flashed yellow. "Put her down."

No one moved.

"I said, put her down!" Cerise sprang from the stream bank onto the bridge, an impossibly high leap. The crowds on both sides of the stream gasped in shock. Cerise crouched on the lip of the bridge as if prepped to pounce.

"Down," she said again.

The many hands let Raven slip, and she landed on the bridge's wooden planks.

"Cerise, how are you doing that?" someone asked.

"Raven Queen was right," said Cerise. "We *can* write our own destiny. And I'm not hiding anymore. I'm proud of both my parents—Red Riding Hood *and* Big Badwolf."

She stood to her full height and pushed back her hood, revealing her wolf ears.

Almost drowned out by both clans' shouts of fear and rage were Cerise's mother's soft cries.

CHAPTER 6

MADDIE ~~CATCHES UP WITH~~  THE NARRATOR

Sneezes at

Narrator? Oh, Narrator, you sweetie crumb cake you?

Maddie, you know I'm not supposed to talk to you.

Yes, but I'm lonely. The school is empty, and everyone else is still off having adventures for Yester Day.

So why did you come back early?

Well, Neverland was nothing like Wonderland. For one thing, there wasn't a single talking rabbit! And I was waylaid by pirates, which should be fun, but they didn't break into any choreographed musical numbers. And...well...ah-ah-achoo! I couldn't stop sneezing. Is it possible to be allergic to pirates? Never mind. Of course it's possible. Everything is possible and nothing is not possible except possibly the impossible. Anywhy, no one there drinks tea, the mermaids splashed me and made fun of my hair, but, worst of all, my friends weren't there.

I'm sorry your Yester Day wasn't satisfactory, Maddie, but I really do need to get back to telling the story.

Ooh, please do, I love stories. Any more juicy secrets like Cerise being part wolf?

Um...besides the Ashlynn and Hunter thing?

Ah-ha, so they are sweet on each other! Tea-rrific!

You didn't know that already? Curses. Well, I'm not saying anything else.

Okay, I'll just start guessing things, and then you freak out if I'm right.

I never freak out.

Is Baba Yaga in love with Headmaster Grimm?

That's ridiculous.

Is Madam Maid Marian a dragon in disguise?

Maddie…

Okay, jump ahead then. Tell me what happens in, like, a hundred pages or something.

Never! Is that how you read books, jumping forward and reading the ending first?

Of course!

Well, there are some things you are better off not knowing beforehand.

Oooh! So something bad is going to happen?

I didn't say that.

To whom? Raven?

No, I wasn't talking about Raven. Just calm down.

Apple?

Never mind about Raven and Apple. And that's all I'm saying, because I will not be tricked into telling you your future, Maddie.

Me?! The big bad thing is going to happen to me?

I didn't say... I was only... you didn't hear it from me, I mean... *argh!*

CHAPTER 7

A Smile and a Friend

To the Hextreme!

APPLE WALKED AWAY FROM HER MOST recent castle while scrolling through the Yester Day app. All she wanted was a monarch who had to deal with super-spazzy subjects who yelled and threw food at one another and yet figured out how to make them stop and just be happy.

After Old King Cole and Empress Buff, she'd rushed a visit to every single available Royal, including three separate branches of the various Charming clans; Briar's mom, Sleeping Beauty (who napped through most of the interview); and

Briar's aunt, that other Beauty, who had married a transformed Beast.

Well, there *was* one more left.

SNOW WHITE. SUBMIT.

Home! Apple's blue eyes sharpened with tears. She hopped out of the wishing well and ran into the White palace, shouting out, "Hello, Cassandra!" and "Good afternoon, Dumpy!" and "Why, thank you, Zelda, plenty of fresh water and exercise do wonders for the complexion."

Soon, Apple was racing into her mother's library, her arms open.

"Apple!" Snow White said. Or rather, squeaked. The original Fairest One of All had spent so much time lost in the woods talking with squirrels her voice never did lower again into its natural range.

Mother and daughter embraced and spoke quickly. Apple had been hexting her all the alarming details of what Raven did on Legacy Day, so she had to fill her in on only the latest. Snow wore her ebony hair in a braided crown. In contrast to her dark hair, her pale skin seemed even paler, her cheeks revealing the barest of blushes. Her dark eyes were as gentle as a doe's, her red-lipped smile near constant.

A gaggle of smiling servants brought milk and cookies, and when they were alone, Apple asked Snow her Yester Day question.

"Trouble?" said Snow. "You know, I haven't had trouble, not since your father kissed me right out of that poisoned sleep. And I never *really* worried, because I knew that, eventually, everything would end up Happily Ever After."

Apple nodded. She used to be able to count on her destiny, too. But that security had been ripped away.

"Even so, there *were* dark times," said Snow White. "I lived with the Evil Queen, after all. And she...didn't like me much."

Snow shivered, and crumbs of her cookie fell to the floor. A flock of bluebirds swooped through the window, pecked up the crumbs, and tweeted.

Snow White laughed, a sound like tinkling glass. "Why, thank you, my feathered friends."

The birds sang a few notes and flew away again.

"But whenever things were too hard for me, I could always find help. Kind servants at Queen Castle. The Huntsman. The dwarves. Most people are genuinely good, sweetheart, and even the evil ones have some good in them. Everyone needs a smile and a friend, whether they know it or not."

Apple paused in her note-taking. "What about the Evil Queen? Did she need a smile and a friend?"

Snow sighed, her expression clouding a little. "Her most of all, I think." Snow bowed her head. "You know, sweetheart, I blame myself a little."

"For the Evil Queen being evil? What? That's silly!"

"Her being evil was just part of the story. But the rest of it—how she went from kingdom to kingdom spreading hate and fear, poisoning poor little Wonderland—it was...terrible." Snow's voice broke with sorrow.

Apple put a hand on her mother's arm.

"No, Mother, that wasn't your fault."

"What if I'd been a friend to her? That wasn't part of the story, but nothing says I couldn't have tried. Or tried harder, anyway. Maybe if she'd had any kind of a friend to stand beside her, Wonderland might still be there."

"It's still there. Just poisoned. Someone will figure out a way to fix it."

Snow looked at her daughter with kind eyes. "Who?" she asked.

"I don't know," said Apple. "Someone?"

Snow took her daughter's hand. "That's the sort of effort that would need a leader. Someone to take charge. But there's no story about someone fixing Wonderland, and in Ever After, if there's no story, it rarely happens. As much as I love this place, that's one thing that's always troubled me. Just a little."

Apple nodded. Perhaps that's why Ever After did have such a hard time stopping the Evil Queen. The moment someone went off script, no one knew what to do. An unscripted crisis was *pure* evil!

"But don't you believe it will turn out all right in The End? What about Legacy Day? What about my destiny?"

"I want you to have your Happily Ever After," said her mother. "More than anything! And the loss of the Snow White story would be catastrophic. But I don't know what will fix everything." She squeezed Apple's hand. "Still, you're right. I have hope. And people are good. *You* are good. And, you know, Raven was always the sweetest little girl."

Snow sighed, blinked, and smiled. Sunlight seemed to fill the room again. Apple could never feel sad for long, not in the presence of Snow White.

"Leadership, Apple. Every effort, group, and kingdom needs a leader its members can look up to."

"But how do you lead those who don't want to be led? How do you do it when it's really hard?"

"The key is…" Snow whisper-squeaked.

Apple leaned in. "Yes?"

"The key is…" Snow leaned closer, too. Her red lips parted, showing her perfectly white teeth. "To keep smiling."

"What?" said Apple. Surely her mother couldn't be suggesting that a smile could solve everything.

"All look to you," said Snow. "If you're smiling, then others will believe that everything is okay."

"But…but if everyone is angry and throwing food and shouting?"

"You just keep smiling."

"Even when you get smacked in the face with porridge?"

Snow laughed and nodded. "Especially then. And when they look to you, just you remember to look back."

"You mean…like, make eye contact?" Apple asked.

Snow smiled and nodded, the corners of her eyes crinkling happily.

Ever After High was in turmoil, and her mother's advice was to smile and make eye contact?

She doesn't understand. The thought scalded in Apple like too-hot porridge. Her mother had never had to deal with anything serious, not outside the events of her own story.

"Keep a confident smile, Apple," said Snow. "And when you look back, look deeper. I mean, more than—"

Suddenly a dwarf bustled up to her mother's elbow.

"Your Majesty, so sorry to interrupt," said the dwarf.

"It's perfectly fine, Achey," Snow said, smiling. "What seems to be the trouble?"

Achey glanced at Apple and then at Snow. "The *finch* is back."

"Oh dear," said Snow. "And the cooks?"

"They're hoping you would, you know, sing it out?" said Achey.

"Of course, of course," Snow said. "I'm sorry, dear. Call me later?"

"Sure," said Apple, feeling her shoulders slump.

Apple shuffled back to the wishing well, accosted by a strange, creeping sensation that wanted to pull her down to the ground. She named it *epic failure*. She hexted Briar Beauty.

APPLE: Where r u?

Briar hexted her coordinates. Apple loaded them into the Yester Day app and entered the wishing well.

She emerged onto unfamiliar terrain. The ground was soft and misty, as if a heavy fog was rolling in, even though the sky was huge above her and as blue as Poppy O'Hair's latest hairstyle. Apple could see no mountains, no forest, just one lone tree.

"Apple!" Briar flung herself at her friend, squeezing her tight. "I'm so glad you're joining me!"

"Are you visiting someone around here?" Apple asked. She wasn't wearing her glasses, and she couldn't see anyone in the strange landscape.

"Nope," said Briar, fiddling with some new kind of belt. "I already visited all the fairytale characters who sleep through part of their story—your mom, my mom, my grandma, Rip Van Winkle. The last three dozed off after two minutes flat, so I had the rest of the afternoon free to practice for the HeXtreme Games!"

Apple was about to ask what the HeXtreme Games were, but she was distracted by Briar's belt. It was hot pink, strappy, and buckled not only around her waist but over her shoulders and between her legs. Apple thought it made her skirt bunch up weirdly, but Briar was always on the cusp of new trends, so Apple trusted it was completely fashionable.

"How was your day? Tell me everything!" said Briar.

"Well, I don't want to complain," Apple began.

"Oh, go ahead and complain. That's why you have a best friend forever after."

"Well, I visited a bunch of royalty, searching for answers about how to lead the students of Ever After High through this crisis, but it turns out no one has really faced an unscripted crisis of their own."

"Uh-huh," said Briar, strapping one of those odd belts around Apple now.

"The only real crises were the ones in their stories, and the stories told them how to get out of it. And their subjects never rose up against them, because that wasn't part of the story. But since Raven broke everything on Legacy Day, we don't have the safety of our destinies anymore. *Anything* could happen, and no one knows what to do about it."

"Right," said Briar, buckling the bits over Apple's shoulders.

"So I went to ask my mom's advice, but she said, 'Keep smiling and make eye contact,' as if that's the answer to everything."

"*Totally* disenchanting," Briar said, running the belt beneath Apple and up her back.

"And so I just feel…like a damsel in distress." Apple stuck out her bottom lip and blew a lock of hair out of her eyes.

Briar held on to Apple's shoulders and stared at her with intense brown eyes. "Everything will work out Happily Ever After. You've always believed that. Just believe."

Apple wanted to believe, but she was distracted by that lone tree. Broad, bright green leaves, thick green trunk. Now that Apple thought about it, it wasn't a tree at all so much as the top of…

Apple grabbed the belt thingy at her waist. No. No, it couldn't be.

"Briar…" said Apple. "Where are we?"

Apple heard a click behind her as Briar snapped a brass hook to the back of her belt thingy.

"No," said Apple, trying to struggle out of the belt that she now realized wasn't a belt at all. "No, no, no, not again…"

She spotted the stretchy, bungee vine leading from the hook on the back of her harness, along the cloudy ground, and back to the top of the tree/beanstalk.

"No," Apple said, but she could manage only a whisper.

"Come on," said Briar. "One bungee jump and you'll forget to be blue!"

Briar grabbed Apple's hand, ran, and leaped through a hole in the clouds, tugging Apple after her.

And suddenly Apple was falling, the clouds left up above her, the Beanstalk a rush of bright green beside her, the wind a slap against her face.

"*Hextreeeeeme!*" cried Briar.

"*Aaaaaaahhhh!!!*" screamed Apple.

CHAPTER 8

TIME TO TAKE OFF THE HOOD
and Put On the Wolf

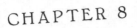

"BANISH HER! BANISH HER!"

The words struck out from both the Hood clan and the Wolf clan like thrown stones.

Raven felt sick. Banishment was the most severe punishment in all of Ever After. Banishment meant Cerise could never again go home to Hood Hollow. Her family *could* live elsewhere, but all fairytale characters were magically tied to their setting. Raven just didn't feel right whenever she was away from Queen Castle for too long. Losing home forever? It was unthinkable! Even beneath Maddie's constant amusement and merriment ran a quiet sadness that she was lost from her setting, unable to go home to Wonderland.

"No, no, no!" Red Riding Hood ran onto the bridge, eyes thick with tears, but voice confident. "No! Banishment must be a unanimous vote, and as a member of the Hood clan, I will *never* vote for it!"

An old woman in a long nightgown, lacy nightcap, and spectacles raised her wrinkled hand. The crowds quieted for whom Raven guessed could only be Grandma. *The* Grandma.

"It's true enough, what Red says," said Grandma, offering Cerise a sad smile. "And I don't like the thought of banishing a member of my own family. But no denying this is serious business. The Evil Queen went off script—and look what happened there."

As one, the entire Hood and Wolf clans shuddered.

"No, sir and ma'am, no good comes from going off script," said Grandma. "This isn't Cerise's fault, but the laws are clear. She is the result of her parents' abandoning their destiny, and if the people vote her out, she cannot remain."

"But—" Red started.

Grandma raised her hand again. "But banishment

is also serious business. What do you say, Cried Wolf?" she asked, turning to the wolf-were. "How about we settle the dispute with a good old-fashioned Basket Run trial?"

Cried Wolf growled but nodded. "The winner will decide Cerise's fate."

"A basket what?" Raven whispered.

"All right, people and canines, you know the rules," said Grandma. "We start at the village, go down the forest path, and end at my house. The first Hood to cross the finish vine still holding a basket wins. If no basketed Hood manages to finish, then whichever Wolf snatches the most baskets wins. The winner decides the fate of our young Cerise." Grandma looked at Cerise and clucked, shaking her head. "Doesn't seem right to banish one so young, but there are laws to uphold."

She said it as if Cerise's fate were already determined, and Raven supposed it was. Looking over the scowling faces, Raven had no doubt that whoever won—Hood or Wolf—would vote to banish Cerise.

Unless Red won the race. The odds weren't in her favor, though—there were a dozen Wolfs and a hundred other Hoods.

The Hoods began stretching their hamstrings, jogging in place. Some Wolfs shot up into human-ish form, others staying canines, pacing back and forth.

"Hext your father," Red whispered to Cerise. "He has a better chance of winning than I do."

"The game begins as soon as I give the signal from my watchtower," Grandma declared.

Cerise was tapping on her MirrorPhone. "Wait—!"

"We have to move fast, dearie," Grandma said to Cerise, and then, leaning in, whispered, "before things really turn big bad." She started to walk. "Each team, pick a coach to join me in the watchtower."

The elderly Brother Hood and white-haired Cranky Wolf volunteered.

"I want to compete, too!" Cerise said, still quickly typing on her phone. "I want a say in my own fate."

"You don't fit on either team, dearie," said Grandma.

"Then I'll be my own team," said Cerise. "And Raven Queen will represent me in the tower."

Grandma and the two coaches huddled in conference. The Wolf and the Hood were shouting, angry, but Raven heard Grandma say, "Nothing in the rules specifically against it. You've got to let her."

"If you let her compete," Raven shouted, "and she loses, you can throw me in the river!"

The two coaches grunted agreement. Grandma waved Raven forward and continued to walk briskly away.

Raven hurried after the three down a long, narrow forest path, monstrous trees guarding the darkness on either side. They reached Grandma's cottage and climbed a ladder to the top of a spindly tower. The platform gave Raven a view of the entire path all the way back to Hood Hollow.

"The girl is an abomination," said Brother Hood.

Cranky Wolf growled. "This is the first time we agree on anything. And it will be the last."

"Shush up, you two," said Grandma, handing them each a megaphone.

"Can I get a megaphone, too?" Raven asked.

"There isn't an extra one," said Grandma. "You'll just have to shout."

Shout? There was no way Cerise would be able to hear her.

Raven slipped her hand into her sleeve and turned on her MirrorPhone. As far as she knew, hexting Cerise wasn't against the rules, but who knew what the others in that watchtower would do to prevent Cerise from winning.

RAVEN: turn on your phone's audio hexting and put phone in your hood pocket so you can hear what I hext you, k?

Cerise was so far away Raven couldn't see if she did as Raven asked.

"On your marks," Grandma shouted into her mega-phone, "get set, and run for your lives!"

The Hoods had the advantage in numbers. The hundred villagers came rushing down the forest path, all equipped with one basket over their arms. In the far back, Raven spotted a red cloak—it was Cerise, darting through the crowd, trying to make it forward. The Hoods seemed to be working against her, purposefully keeping her pinned behind.

"That's right, keep it up!" Brother Hood yelled into the megaphone. "Nice and straight, don't trample each other."

At first Raven couldn't see any Wolfs, but here and there she spotted dark shadows sliding through the forest. Apparently their starting point had been back in the woods, and they ran perpendicular to the path to intercept the Hoods.

"Incoming Wolfs!" Brother Hood shouted.

"Hoods at twelve o'clock!" Cranky Wolf bellowed into his megaphone.

And the first Wolf erupted from the trees. He was monstrously huge, bright gray with a long, toothy snout in full snarl. He tackled the Hood man who was running in front. There was a brief wrestle, and the Wolf came away with the man's basket. The Wolf howled in triumph. The man sat on the ground. He was out.

"That's it, Horribus!" said Cranky. "Now, step out of bounds and get another one!"

Horribus Wolf entered the forest on the other side of the path, ran a ways in, and then pivoted back, emerging again onto the path to tackle a second Hood.

Even the human-form Wolfs were hairy and scary, with large ears the better to hear Hoods with, wide eyes the better to see Hoods with, and sharp teeth the better to bite clean through a basket handle. The Wolfs crisscrossing the path took basket after basket after basket. Still, there were so many Hoods,

Raven wasn't sure the Wolfs could basket-tag them all before someone managed to cross the finish vine. It would be close.

Despite the tackles and growls and howls and shouts, Raven had a strong suspicion that both the Hoods and the Wolfs were enjoying themselves. It was a shame, she thought, that they couldn't let go of the old hatred and suspicion or they'd probably play this game for fun.

She strained to see Cerise, who was still running at the back of the Hood clan, unable to break through.

Grandma smiled, revealing toothless gums. "I love good competition. I tell ya, I don't care if a Hood or a Wolf wins, so long as the game is fierce and dirty."

A Hood or *a Wolf*, Raven thought. *They won't let Cerise win as a Hood. Even if she crosses the finish vine first, they'll claim her win unfair because she has Wolf blood....*

Raven hexted Cerise without looking, not even a glance at her hand. Jack would have been impressed.

RAVEN: need to win both ways. snatch the most baskets & reach finish first. because ur both wolf & hood.

Cerise didn't hext back. Probably because she was vaulting over a woman to escape a pursuing Wolf. But she raised her arm, as if waving to Raven, entered the forest at the side of the path…

And disappeared. Raven smiled. That cloak of Cerise's gave her the ability to slide between shadows. Hexcellent. At least the Wolfs couldn't spot her when she was in the forest.

And Hoods never entered the forest. After all, there were Wolfs in there. And now Cerise was one of them.

Then suddenly Cerise left the woods and streaked across the path. She leaped onto a Hood's shoulders, knocking him to his knees, ripped the basket from his arm, and fled again.

This happened several more times: Cerise's darting from the shadows of the forest, tackling a Hood, taking the basket, and escaping back into the shadows.

But the seventh time, someone followed her.

RAVEN: wolf on ur tail!

Immediately, Cerise turned back, vaulting over

the head of Horribus Wolf. She was struggling to keep hold of ten baskets.

On the path, a Wolf snatched the last basket from the last remaining Hood. Cerise was dodging in and out of the forest, pursued by Horribus. The rest of the Wolfs surged down the path toward the finish vine. Raven quickly counted baskets.

RAVEN: u have the most bskts
RAVEN: run run run

Cerise left the forest and ran, a streak of red hood. The Wolfs howled and chased her. Horribus threw himself forward, reaching for her cape.

RAVEN: jump

Cerise jumped, launching herself forward, and Horribus narrowly missed. She was ahead of the pack, the howls and nips and growls on her heels. Raven had never seen anyone run so fast. *Cerise should seriously go out for Track and Shield.*

Horribus howled. A pack of wolves pounced. And Cerise ran just a little faster. She broke the finish vine in two, her arms full and rattling with baskets.

"I'm the first Hood to break the vine," she said, breathing heavily. "*And* I'm the Wolf with the most baskets. I decide my own fate."

Cranky Wolf and Brother Hood started to protest, but Grandma raised her hand.

"Have any of you ever seen a Basket Run as hex-citing as that? Ever?"

The vanquished Hoods and beaten Wolfs shook their heads.

Grandma laughed and slapped her knee. "By my spectacles, that was something else, girl! You showed us what you're made of, sure enough. Baskets of scones, you sure showed us."

Red Riding Hood stumbled forward, her clothes dusty with dirt. She put out her arms and embraced Cerise.

"What's going on here?" a low voice bellowed.

Mr. Badwolf, Raven's General Villainy teacher, came running down the path. He stopped short. "Cerise! Your hood!"

He indicated her exposed head, and she shrugged.

"It's okay, Dad," she said.

Mr. Badwolf looked around, but no one was surprised to hear her call him Dad. Beneath his long hair and heavy beard, his eyes widened, his mouth opened.

"You mean…"

"They know. We held a Basket Run trial. And I won. I will not be banished."

"I demand a recount!" Horribus Wolf growled.

Raven had followed Grandma down the watchtower ladder and heard her whisper now to Red, "You should go, before things turn ugly. I'll try to soothe the snarls."

While the Hoods and the Wolfs held a basket recount, Raven and Cerise's family hurried away. They settled in the still-dark house behind the closed curtains. Red brought out mini pecan pies. For a time no one spoke. And then Mr. Badwolf asked, "You beat them all?"

Cerise nodded.

"Ten baskets," said Red. "And she broke the vine."

Mr. Badwolf smiled, sharp teeth peeking out. And then he laughed. He laughed so hard he howled, and Cerise joined in.

Mr. Badwolf told Raven about how, when Cerise was a baby, they had to wrap all the chair legs with rubber to keep her from gnawing on the wood. Cerise told them how tired she was of pulling back at school—running slower, throwing shorter, trying to hide her wolf-enhanced abilities. Red tucked a lock of white-streaked black hair behind Cerise's wolf ear and smiled as if she was just as full of love as the pies were full of pecans.

And Raven was both happy and sad. Happy for Cerise and her family. And yet missing now more than ever a mother who could with a smile say how much she loved her. And a family that could sit around a table eating pie and feel content just being together.

Raven had never known that kind of a mother, that kind of a family. Still, she missed the one she had.

She pulled out her MirrorPhone and snapped a picture of Cerise with her dad and mom. Maybe the Hoods and the Wolfs would get used to the idea, and this family photo could be framed and hung on their wall for anyone to see. Maybe someday soon.

"I don't want to hide anymore," said Cerise. "I finally feel free."

Red looked at Mr. Badwolf, who shook his shaggy head.

"Dad, please," said Cerise.

"If Headmaster Grimm found out, things could get a lot worse," said Mr. Badwolf. "I could lose my job for going off script, but even worse, your mother and I could be banished along with you."

Cerise hung her head.

The alarm on Raven's MirrorPhone beeped.

"We have to be back at school in fifteen minutes! And I haven't visited the Candy Witch yet. Thanks, Mrs. Hood, Mr. Badwolf, but I've gotta go!"

She darted out the back door.

"Raven!" Cerise chased her. And caught up easily because, well, she was Cerise. "Raven, you are so awesome. Thanks for helping me stay hidden...." She put her hood up. "For now."

"But"—Raven gestured to the village—"won't the news get out?"

"Hopefully not soon, not till my dad is ready," Cerise said. "Hood Hollowers never talk to 'outsiders,' and most of them don't have MirrorPhones, since they don't trust all this 'newfangled magic.' So we've got time."

"If anyone hears, it won't be from me," said Raven. "Your secret is safe."

"It better be," Cerise said with a smile, "or I will huff and puff and, I don't know, blow your house in. Or something."

"Can you do that?" Raven asked, impressed.

Cerise shrugged. "Probably. Huffing and puffing is in my DNA."

Cerise hesitated, then lurched forward, gave Raven a stiff hug, and fled back into the house.

Raven called after her. "Everything will be okay!"

She wasn't sure that was true, thinking of food fights and Headmaster Grimm and Wolfs tackling Hoods. But she hoped it was true. If things could start to turn around in Hood Hollow, maybe change was possible at Ever After High, too. And if this family could be fixed, maybe her own could be, too. Raven shook her head, not willing to think about things that might just make her sad.

She started the travel app, jumped into the well, and popped back out in a remote part of the Dark Forest, which bore as much resemblance to the Enchanted Forest near the school as Baba Yaga did to Cinderella. Here, the trees were so tall they blocked out all sunlight, the needles on the evergreens a dim grayish green. Raven ducked as she walked to avoid the clutches of tentacle vines. A skinny squirrel scurried past, pausing just to hiss at her.

Beyond the wishing well waited an edible house. Clear sugar-pane windows, gingerbread walls, a taffy roof slowly stretching down, the eaves and windows outlined with colorful candy drops and striped mints. A few bites were missing around the edges, and rain had left pockmarks on the snickerdoodle roof tiles. A spider had spun a large, sticky web in the crook of a candy cane.

"Company!" An old woman threw open the graham cracker door. She wore a floppy black baker's hat over her green hair, but her dress was powder pink and tied in back with a huge bow. The witch seemed to notice Raven's gaze, and she smoothed her skirt.

"I thought this outfit might be less intimidating for company than a witchy wardrobe. I don't get a lot of visitors. I can't imagine why. Come in, precious, come in!"

Raven knew the witch's daughter, Ginger, from school, and she was spella nice, not to mention a wicked good baker. Ginger's mother couldn't be as creepy as the story made her out to be.

"I'm sorry I can't stay long," said Raven, following

her to the door. "Do you mind if I jump right in with a question? I've always been curious—how did you escape the oven after Gretel pushed you in?"

"Keep a rear exit on your oven, Miss Queen," said the Candy Witch. "That's my advice to fellow villains."

Raven frowned. Didn't that count as going off script? Hansel and Gretel's witch was supposed to die in the story. Perhaps variations on the story were okay so long as they happened off the page. Then again, Red and Badwolf's marriage had been off the page.

"Also, work on your cackle," said the witch. "A good cackle and a good oven escape hatch will pay you back in spades."

She cackled long and loud, then stopped suddenly, cocked her head, and asked, "Would you say you'd serve up better roasted with onions or simmered in a nice cream sauce?"

Raven gulped.

The witch cackled again. "I'm kidding! I'm kidding! Or am I...? Ha, you should see your face!"

"Um...may I ask: Why was it okay that you changed your story's ending when you escaped the oven but others couldn't? For example, if after the ball, Cinderella fell in love with the footman and ran off—"

The Candy Witch had just eaten a handful of peppermints, and she choked, spitting them out. "What? Never! Look, if I hadn't lived, I couldn't have had my own sweet Ginger, who will follow her destiny and become the next witch for Hansel and Gretel. Variations work, so long as they help the stories get retold as close to the original as possible."

"I see," said Raven, though she still didn't quite. It didn't seem fair that some people could alter their stories while others were trapped.

"Come into the kitchen." The witch's voice dropped low, rasping in her throat. "I'll show you the *oven*."

"I think I should...stay outside...."

"Though, seriously," the witch asked, tapping the wart on her chin and looking Raven up and down, "do you fit in a large roasting pan?"

It was then that the app alarm thankfully beeped.

CHAPTER 9

A Children's Treasury 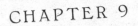 of Fairytale Heirlooms

"Apple! You look..." Raven hesitated, as if trying to find the right word. "You look...*alarmed.*"

Apple turned to the full-length mirror beside her wardrobe. Her golden hair was perfectly curled. Her round cheeks were perfectly blushed. Her cropped jacket and dress were perfectly tidy. But her expression was sort of stuck, as if she'd been recently screaming in terror.

"Yes, I ran into Briar," said Apple. "On a cloud.

At the top of the Beanstalk. On the wrong end of a bungee vine."

"Ah," said Raven.

They both stood there. Apple checked her fingernails. Raven squinted at a freckle on her arm.

"So, um, how was your Yester Day?" asked Raven.

"Well, I got to visit my mom," said Apple.

"That's nice," said Raven. "That must be nice to get to visit her, you know, whenever you want."

"It is," Apple sighed. "But . . . well, I was supposed to come back with all my questions answered and the knowledge of how to fix this mess."

"Yeah, me too," Raven said, sitting on her bed.

Apple sat beside her. "Well . . . you *could* tell all your Rebel friends that you made a mistake and you want to follow your destiny after all."

Raven rolled her eyes.

"Raven, without destiny, we get chaos!" said Apple. "Did you know that until yesterday, Ever After High Castleteria had never suffered through a single food fight? I looked it up."

"Destiny prevents *freedom*," said Raven. "And without freedom, how can anyone really be happy?"

"Destiny *is* freedom," said Apple. "Freedom from

worry and uncertainty. Lasting happiness comes from following our destiny."

"I tried to follow my destiny for years, Apple. I tried to be evil for my mother's sake, but I wasn't happy doing it."

"Oh, Raven…" Apple frowned. "You know, not one of the royals I visited today knew how to handle an unexpected situation. Happy or not, all of us are lost without destiny. And look at your mother. The Evil Queen went against destiny and took down Wonderland with her—and almost all of Ever After, too! Her rampage cost her her freedom and her life, and you lost your mother. By rebelling, she wasn't just playing an evil role. She became the much more frightening destiny-less kind of evil. You say you don't want to be evil like her, but by denying your destiny aren't you following in her exact evil footsteps?"

"I…I don't know…"

"Um…that was a rhetorical question," Apple said helpfully. "The answer is yes. Yes, denying your destiny is following in her exact evil footsteps."

"This isn't a pop quiz, Apple. It's my life."

"And *my* life," said Apple. "My destiny. And

everyone else's, too. Without the security of destiny, people get afraid. And when they're afraid—"

"They throw porridge and pies," said Raven. "I know. And I'm sorry. There has to be a way to rebel, to make our own choices, without hurting anyone."

"I couldn't find any answers today. No royal has ever faced unscripted things like food fights and angry mobs and chaos."

Raven's lips lifted into a half smile. "Well, except…"

Apple perked up. "Who? You know someone? I'm willing to talk to *anyone*."

"Nobody, nothing," Raven said, shaking her head. "Sorry."

They sat in silence for a moment.

"You were going to say your mother, weren't you?" Apple said, her voice a whisper.

Raven looked up, eyes wide. "What? That, um, that's not possible, you know, because she's—"

"Gone forever," Apple said. "I know it's probably horrible for you, not just to have had an evil mom, but to have to deal with her being…oh drat, I shouldn't even be talking about this, should I? It probably just comes across as my being mean again. Sorry."

"It's okay," Raven said.

"You're right, though. She certainly would have very different advice than any of the other Royals I spoke to!"

Raven groaned.

"There I go again," Apple said. "You know, I think of myself as a sensitive person, but I just keep saying these things! Though, if she were here, I bet she'd guide you toward embracing your evilness."

Raven stiffened. "You don't know what you're talking about."

"It's funny, isn't it," Apple went on, "that the Evil Queen and I would give you the exact same advice?"

"She was a rebel," said Raven. "She'd want me to rebel."

"Not from your destiny. She'd want you to be evil."

"What is being evil, though, really? Doing what people don't like? If that's true, then I'm right there!"

"Being evil is like her," said Apple, "and what she did in the Snow White story. Do that."

"Yeah, okay, she wants me to be like her," Raven said, standing. "But she also told me to give 'em hex, and to face Legacy Day head-on, brave and powerful, and show everyone what I'm made of. And what I'm made of is not evilness!"

"What do you mean?" Apple rose slowly. "What do you mean, she *wants* you to be like her? She told you all this when you were a little girl, right? She was talking to you about Legacy Day long ago, when you were little, before she died. Because she *is* gone forever, right, Raven?"

Raven clenched her jaw and looked away.

"Raven?" Apple said.

"I'm so sick of secrets," Raven whispered. "I'm with Cerise. Secrets really huff and puff."

"Raven, please, you're kind of freaking me out. Just tell me that your mother is gone."

Raven looked at Apple, and Apple had the distinct impression that Raven was readying herself to lie. But then her shoulders slumped, and Raven bowed her head and said, "I can't do that, Apple."

"Wait wait wait! What?" Apple backed away, looking around in terror. "Was that a joke?"

"No, she never died to begin with. Headmaster Grimm told everyone that so they wouldn't worry, and I'm not supposed to tell. So you can't tell anyone else, please. She's actually in mirror prison. As a fan of security, you'd like it. No one's ever escaped from mirror prison."

Apple slowly sat back down, but the knowledge of the Evil Queen's continued existence gave her cackling chills.

"Whoa," said Apple. "The original Queen of Chaos. Alive."

"You know, she *was* the most rebellious of rebels," said Raven. "When everything was totally off-script—even though it *was* her own doing—she still managed to rule a kingdom and make her people love her and follow her. I bet she'd have advice for both of us on a Yester Day visit."

"You aren't suggesting…you don't mean…we couldn't *really* visit her, could we?" Apple asked, her voice shaking.

"Hex no, we only get one yearly MirrorChat, and we already had it. I was, you know, thinking out loud. Pretend it was a joke."

Apple's eyes widened. And then she forced a laugh. "Yes. Funny. Evil Queen is alive. Let's chat with her. Great joke. Good times."

A loud knock on their door startled Apple. The door slammed open and Cerise hurried inside.

"Raven, you should come. There's something going on."

Raven and Apple both ran after Cerise—barely keeping up. They began to hear shouts.

"You shouldn't be in there!"

"Get out or you'll get us all in trouble!"

Cerise led them down a flight of stairs and around the corner from the Muse-eum. A crowd of students was gathered outside a room Apple had only heard of before. The door resembled the cover of a book, the title engraved in the wood: A CHILDREN'S TREASURY OF FAIRYTALE HEIRLOOMS.

The massive steel lock was open, and the door was ajar.

Apple's classmates stood in the hall, looking through the open door.

"I didn't mean to," Blondie Lockes said as soon as she saw Apple. "I just touched the lock, it fell off, and the door swung open."

Apple sighed. Locks just gave up around Blondie. Her mother, Goldilocks, had been the same way, and the Three Bears had installed triple dead bolts.

"You opened the Treasury door?" said Apple. "Who's inside?"

Laughter exploded out.

"Curses," said Raven. "It's Sparrow Hood and his Merry Men."

Blondie stood in the threshold, gazing in. "Ooh, look at all the crowns!"

"Blondie!" said Apple, going after her. As soon as Apple entered, the crowd in the hallway followed.

"Apple, we should get out," said Raven. "We're making it worse."

"No way. I don't trust Sparrow and his crew around these treasures," said Apple. "Why, there's my heirloom glass coffin! Hmmm, it looks a little snug."

"At least there's no food to throw," said Raven.

Sparrow was examining a mannequin dressed in royal robes and adorned with jewels. A placard read: THE EMPEROR'S OLD CLOTHES.

"Oh, hi, Apple," said Sparrow. He slipped a gold ring off one of the mannequin's fingers and began to toss and catch it. "All this talk about destiny has got me thinking. If destiny is as important as you say, then I really should be living up to mine." He slipped the ring into his pocket.

"Aren't you going to stop him?" Raven asked.

"I don't know," said Apple. "It *is* his destiny to steal from the rich and give to the poor."

"I'm sooo poor," Sparrow lamented. "Ooh, good, riches!" He plucked another ring off the statue.

"Sparrow, come on," said Raven.

"Oh, really, Raven Queen? You of all people are going to tell me to follow the rules?"

Raven opened her mouth as if to shout, but she took a big breath and turned away, staying in the Treasury's threshold.

"Maybe I should abandon my destiny, too, just like Raven Queen," said Sparrow. From a pedestal he picked up Dr. King Charming's championship crown from when he was captain of the Dragon-Slaying Squad and put it on his head.

Daring Charming marched in, the crowd parting for him. "Sparrow Hood, don't you dare ruin anything else Royal. You already crowned me with corned beef hash."

"There's jam on your hands, too," said Sparrow. "I saw you throw a berry tart that struck Cupid."

"That was you?" Cupid asked. A lock of her dusty-pink hair was still stained red from the food fight.

But Daring's piercing blue eyes were targeted on Sparrow. "Take off my father's championship crown."

"What's the harm, Your Uppity Royal Highness?" said Sparrow. "Worried that since Raven Queen flipped the script, *I* might end up a king and *you* an outlaw?"

"Impossible! Destiny will still prevail. I, for one, signed the Storybook of Legends!"

"Well, I didn't," said Sparrow. "Who knows how this will all shake out?"

"Indeed," said Kitty Cheshire, shrugging her thick purplish pigtails over her shoulders and adjusting her cat-eared cap. "Maybe Cedar Wood will become a queen."

Kitty took a tiara from a display case, disappeared, and reappeared again behind Cedar, placing the tiara on her head.

"And Prince Dexter Charming?" Kitty smiled hugely. Her smile lingered a moment after she disappeared. She reappeared beside Dexter, holding a broom, which she thrust into his hands. "He might become a wicked witch!"

Dexter looked at the broom, shrugged, and gave

a small laugh, glancing over at Raven as if to check what she thought.

Kitty kept popping in and out, so quickly Apple couldn't follow the movement, but suddenly Pinocchio's puppet strings were tied to Humphrey Dumpty's wrists, the Mad Hatter's top hat was perched on Holly O'Hair's head, Grandma's basket-o-goodies was thrust into Hopper Croakington's hands, and Hansel's petrified breadcrumbs were poured into Lizzie Hearts's pocket.

"Kitty!" said Apple, her hands in fists. Everyone's destiny was at stake. This was not a time for jokes!

"Everything is upside down." Kitty disappeared again. In a moment her smile reappeared, floating in the air but tipped downward like a frown, as if Kitty was dangling from the ceiling headfirst. The frown laughed. "What's the matter, White Apple? Just realized you aren't in control?"

There was a hush in the room, the crowd waiting for Apple to respond. Perhaps to say something leader-ish and make everything all right again. But Apple hesitated. What in Ever After could she do?

Laugh at everything like Old King Cole?

Stomp her foot and scowl like Empress Buff?

Smile and make eye contact like her mother?
Nothing seemed right.

"I...uh..." She always used to know what to say. But she also used to be Apple White, future Snow White and future queen. If Raven broke their tale, who *was* Apple anymore?

The hushed moment passed. With no direction from Apple, the crowd began to talk at once.

"Look, those are the original glass slippers!"

"Maybe I *could* be a Royal now."

"Maybe I wouldn't *have* to be a Royal now."

"Do you think that tiara would fit me?"

"Stop it, you guys," said Apple. "Please."

No one paid her any attention. Anger cooked Apple, and she turned to Raven. "They wouldn't normally act like this, you know. They're all riled up—scared even—after Legacy Day."

"You're saying that this is my fault?" said Raven.

"Well, partly, yes."

"It's not, Apple," said Raven. "It's not all my fault. They choose what they do. I'm not making anyone do anything!"

Apple saw Ashlynn Ella trying on a pair of elf-made shoes, her hands trembling as if she just couldn't help herself. Apple started toward her, intending to rally her Royal friends into setting a good example, but she overheard Ashlynn say, "If I were a shoemaker instead of a princess, then I could marry whomever I wanted."

Hunter Huntsman set down his ax and took up a sword. "What if I'd been born a prince...?"

He looked at Ashlynn. She blushed and turned away, her hand rising to her cheek where she'd been recently smacked with a soy turkey sausage patty.

"I've decided, Ash," Hunter whispered. "I'm giving up on my destiny. I'm going to drop out of school and become a fisherman."

"Hunter, no! For one thing, you're a vegan!"

What? He was supposed to be the Huntsman in the Snow White story, *Apple's* story, not go off and become a fisherman! When had Hunter become unhappy with his destiny? And for that matter, why was Ashlynn dreaming about being a shoemaker instead of a princess? It seemed the catastrophic events of Legacy Day were infecting more people than Apple had realized.

Shouting drew back Apple's attention. While she'd

been eavesdropping on Hunter and Ashlynn, the crowd in the Treasury had lost all control.

Duchess Swan was holding Humphrey's strings and puppeting him around the room. Briar was climbing atop the Princess and the Pea stack of mattresses. Dexter zoomed by, teetering on the witch's broom. A boy in glasses flying around on a broomstick—what a peculiar sight!

"How do witches do this?" Dexter said, wobbling dangerously.

The yelling grew louder, and what had been playful began to turn bad, like a pastry left too long in the oven.

"You Royals be careful with our heirlooms—our stories matter, too, you know."

"Well, you Rebels be careful with ours!"

"Watch out!"

"Put that back!"

"You put yours back!"

"Rebels are so—"

"Well, Royals are incredibly—"

"Vermin!"

"Tyrant!"

"Destiny is mine! Mwa-ha-ha!"

Twice in two days, these groups were shouting, upset, everything as upside down as Kitty Cheshire's smile. And Apple in the middle of it all again, though this time her confidence seemed to have turned into a frog and hopped away.

"Stop," Apple said. But not loud enough to be heard.

She couldn't seem to make eye contact with anyone. And a confident smile slid off her face, leaving her with a heavy and unfamiliar frown.

Apple was afraid. Something worse than detention would come of this. She felt it in her core. And yet she believed herself powerless to stop it.

CHAPTER 10

MADDIE GABS WITH THE NARRATOR

Narrator! Yoodle-hoo! I've been looking for Raven everywhere. I wanted to hear about her Yester Day.

I think she's a little busy right now.

Where, in the Treasury? It's so noisy! I didn't know there was a party going on.

Not a party—

Don't be silly. Look at everyone dancing

around. This must be a party. Though, don't tell Dexter, but falling off a witch's broomstick is an odd way to dance. Why does Sparrow have his pockets stuffed full of—Oh! I see! It's a Swappersnatch Gyre!

It's . . . what?

Oh, you know! Once a year we would invade the Queen of Hearts's castle, take things, and hide them all over Wonderland. The treasure hunt could last for months.

Ah, yes, I learned about the Swappersnatch Gyre in my Advanced Allusions and Cross-Cultural Reference class my last year at Ever After High. But this isn't—

I didn't know Ever After celebrated the Swappersnatch Gyre. What fun!

Maddie, *wait*!

CHAPTER 11

~~The Uni Cairn~~
Run for Your Lives!

RAVEN GLARED. THE NOISE WAS TWISTING her stomach and scratching at her eardrums, and she felt as if she'd landed in a nest full of giant chickens. Stranger things than finding oneself in a nest of giant chickens did occur in Ever After, not least of which was the scene before her.

Helga and Gus Crumb were playing tug-of-war with a piece of Neversnap Taffy. Briar was dozing atop the stack of mattresses, her superpowered sleep allowing her to ignore the pea beneath them, and snoring sweetly. Sparrow and his Merry Men were improvising a truly dreadful rendition of "Stairway to Valhalla" on the Treasury's stock of instruments, including Professor Pied Piper's magic flute, Jack's golden harp, and the Wicked Witch's bongos of madness. And on top of it all were the constant shouts—Rebels and Royals yelling and name-calling and blaming each other.

Raven just wanted to run away. Or at least find a pot of peas porridge to hide behind. But that hadn't done much good last time.

"This has got to stop before something gets broken!" Apple said, backing into the threshold with Raven and away from the bedlam. "Do something, Raven!"

"Me?" said Raven. "I never asked to be a leader, and I don't know how to be one anyway."

"Well, you are, whether you like it or not."

"I tried to stop an angry mob earlier today and nearly ended up in a river. Besides, why don't *you* do something?"

"Do what—smile and make eye contact?" said Apple.

Raven tilted her head. "What?"

"Nothing, never mind. I'm as mad as a hot apple dumpling because I should be able to fix this, but no one had any useful advice for me today and I…I…I don't know what to do!"

"Everybody calm down!" Raven yelled.

Some people glanced her way but kept on with what they were doing.

"They're just choosing their own destiny. Isn't that what you wanted?" said Blondie, wearing a full royal cape and crown.

Raven clenched her fists and felt a crackling in her fingertips. A dozen different spells ran through her head. Could she freeze everyone? Make them levitate? Cover them in sticky goo? Turn them into lizards? That might stop the madness—but then again, the spell could backfire and turn everyone into lizards *permanently*. Or worse.

"Ooh!" Maddie ran in. "A party!"

"Maddie…wait, it's not—" Raven started. But Maddie was already in the middle of the fray, squealing and shouting, "Happy Swappersnatch, everybody!"

The crowd thickened, and Raven could no longer see Maddie. Raven was just about to risk that freeze spell after all when someone yelled, "The headmaster!"

The room emptied faster than a bowl of candy in the hands of Helga and Gus.

Raven moved out of the threshold as Headmaster Grimm, Madam Baba Yaga, and Professor Rumpelstiltskin entered. Only then did Raven realize one person had stayed behind in the Treasury.

Maddie was standing on a giant helmet, which had fallen off a giant suit of armor. Raven could see peeking out of Maddie's skirt pocket the brass tip of Aladdin's lamp and a pink magic wand. On the ground below her, as if it had fallen from her pocket, lay a tiny glass unicorn.

"Wheee!" yelled Maddie. "Don't stop now. Let's party on!"

"Headmaster!" Rumpelstiltskin yelled, pointing at the unicorn. "Is that..."

"The Uni Cairn," the headmaster whispered.

Baba Yaga gasped in fright. It was a sound like the inhale of a dragon, like the hiss of a giant python. A sound Raven never thought to hear from the steely dark sorceress. Was she joking? It was just a mini glass figurine, like the kind one might buy in a souvenir shop for the price of a pack of gum.

"Back! Everyone back!" Headmaster Grimm shouted. "I need a magical perimeter *now*!"

Apple and Raven backed up farther into the threshold. Maddie hopped off the helmet and joined them.

"What is all the fussing and fretting and flustering?" she asked.

Raven shrugged.

The headmaster tiptoed forward, while Baba Yaga and Rumpelstiltskin stepped carefully behind him, holding out their hands, magic sparking between them.

"Is the Uni Cairn...compromised?" asked Baba Yaga.

"What is that thing?" Raven whispered.

"Looks like one of those trinkets I used to collect on my dresser," Apple whispered back.

The headmaster took a magnifying glass from his breast pocket and peered through it.

"Cracked," he said in a strained whisper.

Baba Yaga gasped. Rumpelstiltskin wailed.

"That's what you get for using a glass knickknack!" said Baba Yaga.

"It was the last place anyone would look!" said

the headmaster. "Besides, binding spells are most effective on glass—glass towers, glass slippers, glass mirrors…"

Grimm was rambling, his hands trembling above the trinket.

"Oh dear, you want me to glue your pretty toy?" Maddie asked, taking off her hat and rummaging through it. "I'm sure I have a tube of super duper glooper glue in here some—"

"Stay back!" the headmaster yelled. "No one touch the Uni Cairn! I'll need…let's see…a pillow woven from fairy silk, sterling silver tweezers, and, uh…a drop of charm blossom honey. Oh, and—"

He was interrupted by a quiet *tink*. The glass unicorn had moved. Milton Grimm held up his hands for silence. Raven held her breath. She suddenly felt afraid.

Tink, tink, crick…The microscopic crack in its neck lengthened, and its tiny head clinked off.

"No," Headmaster Grimm breathed.

A wisp of black smoke snaked out of the beheaded neck. The smoke rose, billowing bigger, wider, greater, until it filled half of the huge Treasury. Then, as if someone had turned on a humongous fan, the black cloud gusted away, revealing beneath it an enormous winged monster.

Its body was scaled like a dragon's but its long, clawed hands and feet were ragged with fur. Its eyes were huge and pearly white, its front teeth like some demon rabbit's, and its tail as long as a hundred snakes.

It hissed. Or roared. Or growled. Or shrieked. Or some mix of all four. Its head snapped around, its blind white eyes looked right at Baba Yaga, who was chanting a spell. It hiss/roar/growl/shrieked at her. Baba Yaga shrieked back. The monster flinched, turned, and flew through a window. Only the window was much too small, so technically it flew through the wall.

"Chase it!" shouted Headmaster Grimm.

"It's too late," said Rumpelstiltskin.

"I didn't get a chance to finish my containment spell," Baba Yaga said, her shoulders slumping. "Now that it's gone, there is no hunting it. There is only waiting for it to attack. It will likely go into hiding for years to recuperate. But when it returns, all of Ever After will feel its wrath."

"What *was* that?" Raven asked.

Maddie, Lizzie Hearts, and Kitty Cheshire—the three Wonderlandians—were standing together just outside the Treasury, their backs to the wall, their eyes wide. At the same time, they said, "The jabberwocky."

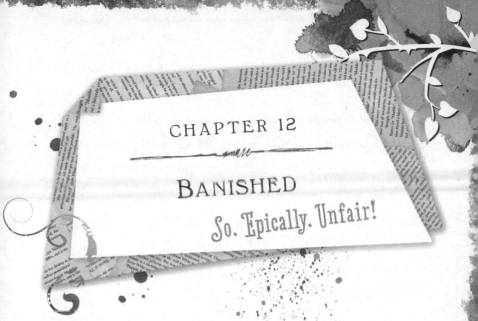

CHAPTER 12

BANISHED

So. Epically. Unfair!

THE NEXT MORNING, TALKING FROGS AWOKE the school. Apple heard the wet slaps of their hops coming down the hall before she heard their voices.

"All students, report to the Charmitorium. *Croooak*. All students to the Charmitorium at once. *Crooooooooak*."

"*Nooo…*" Raven croaked from under her covers, not unlike a talking frog. "It's the weekend. No school today. Must. Sleep. In."

"No sleeping in today," croaked a frog from the corridor.

Apple stretched, dressed, and ran a comb through her golden curls. Raven was still trying to work a brush through her black-and-purple snarls when Apple left to meet up with Blondie and Briar. They sat in their usual high-backed, plush box seats in the Charmitorium.

"Any idea?" Briar asked.

"None," said Apple.

"Oh toadstools," said Blondie. "I was hoping to get an inside scoop."

"I mean," said Apple, "this meeting probably has something to do with how a bunch of students broke into the Treasury last night, turned into a mob, and broke something called a Uni Cairn, which released a terrifying Wonderlandian monster from its tiny, magical prison, but besides that, I have no intel on the specifics."

Though shouldn't she, as a prominent student leader at Ever After High? Apple made eye contact with Maddie, who was sitting next to Raven, Cerise, and Cedar on the wooden benches on the main floor.

Apple tilted her head, asking her co-president a question—did she know what was happening? Maddie shook her head no.

Headmaster Grimm took the stage, looking, Apple thought, *particularly* grim. Baba Yaga, Gepetto, the White Queen, Mother Goose, Rumpelstiltskin, and other members of the senior faculty stood behind him. The White Queen looked extremely pale today, Baba Yaga looked as if she hadn't slept in a decade, and Gepetto was trembling.

"You all know why we're here," Headmaster Grimm said.

Apple could see the heads of students around her go lower as those who'd been in the Treasury the day before cowered in their seats.

"I am not happy, students, not happy with any of you. But one of you especially crossed a line—yes, crossed so far that there's no going back."

Apple assumed the headmaster meant Sparrow Hood. But fear bathed her with an icy chill as she thought—what if he blamed Raven? Her rebellion had incited the students, after all, and she *had* torn the Storybook of Legends. No, he couldn't expel her. If Raven didn't go to Ever After High anymore, Apple could never change her mind and get her back on the right path again!

But instead of Sparrow or even Raven, the headmaster called out, "Come up here now, Madeline Hatter."

There was a general gasp of surprise and alarm.

Maddie stood and made her way down the row. Raven started to go with her, but the headmaster said, "Madeline *alone*, if you please."

Maddie stood on the far end of the stage, twisting the finger of one of her gloves. Her knees knocked, her feet pointed toward each other. Apple had never noticed before how small Maddie was until she saw her there beside the faculty. Apple could see in Maddie's pocket her pet dormouse shivering, his tiny hands gripping the brim of his top hat.

"Yesterday I saw Madeline Hatter in the Treasury, her pockets full of stolen heirlooms. At her feet, clearly just fallen from her hands, the Uni Cairn—one of the Great Glass Prisons. Her carelessness has unleashed the most terrifying horror Wonderland ever knew, now loose in our own Ever After! And I'm not convinced she didn't throw down that glass prison on purpose. It's well known that Madeline Hatter misses her home world. Perhaps she went into the Treasury with the express purpose of setting free one of her countrybeasts, the ... the *jabberwocky*." The headmaster shuddered.

"But—" Maddie started.

"Silence! Your testimony is not needed. It doesn't matter what you meant to do, only what you did. And what you did was free a vastly dangerous, frightening, and *deadly* beast!"

A general shiver passed around the audience. Someone began to weep.

The headmaster raised his hand. "Now, don't be afraid, children. We know from legend that the jabberwocky will hide itself for years, slowly regaining its terrifying powers, before attacking. But when that distant day comes, Madeline Hatter, it will be *your* fault. You committed a crime of Big Bad Proportions—something great, terrible, dangerous, and completely off-script. Your punishment, therefore, can be nothing less than banishment from the land of Ever After. You will leave here and never return."

The students in the audience gasped again, this time with even more alarm. Someone banished!

And not just anyone, but Maddie! Apple couldn't think of anyone else whom all the students—both Royals and Rebels—liked as much as the tea-loving, party-throwing, riddle-spouting girl.

"Thank you, that's very kind," said Maddie, voice quavering. "I appreciate it."

"What are you saying, girl?" said Baba Yaga. "You appreciate getting banished?"

"Oh, no, I find the idea of banishment horrifying, frightening, and generally extremely icky. I was responding to what the Narrator said—that you all like me. It's nice, at least, to know that."

Maddie sniffed, and a fat tear rolled down her cheek.

Apple quaked in her seat but could resist no longer. She stood up. And at the exact same moment, so did Raven.

"Headmaster!" they both said at once.

"Sir, if you'd be so kind as to hear a question?" Apple shouted to be heard across the Charmitorium. "I saw, as you did, Maddie standing near the broken Uni Cairn in the Treasury. We witnessed the moment *after* its break, not its breaking, therefore, any witness testimony is circumstantial at best—"

"Your Royal Highness," said the headmaster. "This is not the time to debate—"

"Anyway, what is one of these so-called Great Glass Prisons doing in the school Treasury?" Raven asked. "Shouldn't you keep it somewhere safer?"

"Such as *behind heavily locked doors?*" Baba Yaga muttered.

"You of all people, Raven Queen," said the headmaster, "have no place to speak up in this matter. You're lucky you're not getting banished, too!"

Raven glanced back at Apple, as if asking for help.

"But Maddie has an explanation, I bet," said Apple, "and if we just listened to her—"

"Madeline Hatter not only meddled with one of the Great Glass Prisons, she broke it!" said Headmaster Grimm. "As such, I am authorized to judge and convict her myself. The only defense for a crime of Big Bad Proportions would be Irrefutable Evidence, something Madeline cannot offer. Therefore, she is banished. I will personally inform her father that she has twenty-four hours to pack and make her good-byes. We will meet by the school wishing well at this time tomorrow morning. There, Baba Yaga will perform the banishment spell, and you will all witness Madeline Hatter depart Ever After forever after."

Neither Apple nor Raven, who were both still standing, seemed to find anything else to say. Their mouths hung open in stunned silence.

Maddie broke the silence. "Um...where am I being banished to?" she asked, her voice a little shaky.

"Wonderland's portal is sealed shut, Maddie," Gepetto said with some warmth in his voice, "or we would send you home. So we decided on the next best thing: Neverland."

The faculty members all nodded. Apple didn't think they noticed how Maddie recoiled at the name.

"Yes, Neverland," said the White Queen, smoothing her shockingly white hair over her white shoulder. "Surely it is the most like Wonderland. After all, they both share the same last name: *Land*."

The headmaster dismissed the school, and immediately the Charmitorium erupted into conversations and shouts of concern. Apple left Blondie and Briar and ran back to the stage door. Raven did the same, so they met Maddie as she came out.

Something was very wrong with Maddie's face. Apple shivered, unsure what had happened. A spell?

A mask? No, she realized. For the first time since she'd met her, Maddie was frowning. It was a sight sorrowful enough to provoke a tear from even a jaded Narrator.

"Maddie," said Raven, reaching out for her hand. "This is unbelievable. I can't...I don't even have words..."

"I've got to go with Mr. Grimm to tell my dad," said Maddie with a sniff. "He'd wonder, you know, if I just disappeared and never came back. Telling your dad that you're getting banished makes sense, doesn't it?"

"None of this makes sense, Maddie," said Apple, squeezing her other hand. "None of it!"

"Oh good," said Maddie. "I didn't think it made sense, either, so I was worried that it probably did to everyone else and I'd just gone mad. Or, madder than normal. I mean...I don't even remember touching the wee, bitty unicorn. I don't *think* I broke it. I thought everyone was celebrating a festival," Maddie sighed. "Maybe I don't belong in Ever After anyway. I've never understood how everything works...."

"Maddie," Raven said, giving her a hug.

Maddie pulled away and smiled, though it

seemed to strain her trembling lips, and her eyes still glistened.

"Don't get gloomy gummy about me. I'll be…I'll be okay. Bubble pop shop," Maddie said, stood on one leg, and jumped forward. "And hop."

She hopped away, shoulders slumped, looking like a disappointed rabbit. Raven started to go after her, but then Baba Yaga emerged from the Charmitorium stage door.

"Madam Baba Yaga," said Raven. "Please, you have to help Maddie. She didn't do it, but if she did do it, she didn't mean to—"

"Miss Queen, a crime of Big Bad Proportions cannot be waved away by whining that the criminal probably didn't mean to do it." Baba Yaga turned to Apple, the tiny bones tied up in her long gray hair clinking together. She stared. Apple felt her scalp crawl, as if it were trying to run away.

"As the headmaster declared," Baba Yaga said, still staring at Apple, "only Irrefutable Evidence could have saved her."

Baba Yaga walked away, though Apple held still as if at attention, just in case the old sorceress had eyes in the back of her head.

Headmaster Grimm entered the corridor. He saw Raven and lowered his eyebrows.

"You see what happens when you don't follow your destiny, Miss Queen? Your friends get hurt. Banished, even. It's enough to make one reconsider one's previous rash decisions." He stalked closer. "If you don't change your mind and make the right choice, I wonder which of your dearest friends will suffer next!"

Raven took a step back, her eyes wide in shock.

"Shameful day, Your Majesty," he said to Apple. "Most unpleasant."

Apple could feel Raven practically vibrating beside her as she watched the headmaster walk away.

"I just made my own choice," Raven said through clenched teeth. "I didn't make anyone do anything. It's not my fault!"

Apple knew Raven hadn't meant harm, but going off script endangered everyone. Now was not the time to say so.... Raven looked as if she was about to explode.

"I feel like I'm about to explode," Raven said, fists clenched and flickering purple.

Apple began to pace. "This is just wrong. I mean,

Maddie is everyone's friend. She's always happy and always helps everyone else to be happy. Without her, *everyone* will be more miserable. And I don't believe she's ever purposefully done something bad. That's why this is so...so *unfair*. I really, really don't like unfairness, Raven. Just thinking about Maddie getting unfairly banished makes me want to...to throw something!"

"Really?" said Raven.

"Or something even worse than throwing," said Apple. "Hitting something? Like, punching a pillow, maybe? I've never done that before, but I feel quite prepared to punch all sorts of pillows. Maddie didn't get a fair trial, not to mention that banishment solves nothing! For one thing, banishing Maddie means she can't grow up to run the Mad Hatter's Haberdashery and Tea Shoppe, and that's another destiny lost, another story that won't get told."

Apple stopped pacing. Raven dropped her fists. They both just looked at each other.

"We need to do something," Apple and Raven said at the same time.

Apple grabbed Raven's hand and pulled. They ran down several flights of stairs and into the library.

Apple pulled the "I" volume of *Auntie Aesop's Complete Compendium of Ever After* from the shelf, and together Apple and Raven carried the twenty-pound tome to the far back corner. Apple flipped it open.

"Irrefutable Evidence is a spell!" Apple whispered, reading. "Headmaster Grimm said the only defense for a crime of Big Bad Proportions is Irrefutable Evidence. Auntie Aesop starts to describe how to do the spell but suddenly changes languages."

Raven took the book from Apple, reading hungrily, then sighed and slammed it shut.

"The spell is written in Cursed Gibberish. It's a magical language."

"And you can read it?" Apple asked, nodding and smiling, her eyes wide and glistening hopefully.

Raven shook her head. "I'm a level-five sorceress. To understand Cursed Gibberish, you have to be level thirty-eight. The only sorceresses I've ever met who are fluent in Cursed Gibberish are Baba Yaga and—"

Raven stopped.

"Well, Baba Yaga will never help us," said Apple. "When she glares at me, it's like every hair on my head stands up and tries to run away."

"There's a rule in dark sorcery anyway," Raven muttered. "Upper-level knowledge can't be down-shared, and Baba Yaga is a faculty member, so she'll definitely follow the rules. The headmaster would never let her anyway. He's furious. I kind of wonder if he's punishing Maddie in part to get back at me for Legacy Day."

"Wait, you said *sorceresses*—like, plural. Who else can read Cursed Gibberish?"

"Um…" Raven said.

"Oh!" Apple said.

For a moment, they were both silent.

"But she does," Raven whispered. "My mother does speak Cursed Gibberish."

Apple tried to laugh. It sounded too much like one of Bo Peep's sheep's bleats. "That's one of your jokes, right? One of your I'm-just-kidding-about-calling-up-my-evil-imprisoned-mother jokes? Ha! Raven, you are so funny."

Raven didn't laugh.

Apple swallowed. "There must be someone else."

Raven hexted the Candy Witch. Her answer was slightly alarming.

CANDY: No, I don't speak Cursed Gibberish,
but I ate someone once who did. I'm kidding!
Or am I? COL!

Apple leaned over to look at Raven's phone.
"COL?" she asked.

Raven groaned. "Cackle out loud," she said. "It's a witch thing."

Raven found *The Official Registry of Witches, Sorceresses, Conjuring Goblins, and Hags* on a back shelf. Nobody else in all of Ever After had reached higher than level thirty-one.

She looked up at Apple, the purples of her eyes bright and serious but nervous, too. Apple shivered.

"She's level thirty-eight?" asked Apple.

"She's level forty-two, actually," said Raven. "And she doesn't care about rules."

Apple shivered again and looked around the library, half expecting to see the specter of the Evil Queen there, leaning over them, her shadow like a creeping plague.

"We need her help, Apple," Raven said. "We need to talk to her."

Apple groaned and covered her head with her arms.

"But I need your help, too, Apple. You're smart. Honestly, you're the smartest person I know."

Apple slumped down in the chair in a very un-Apple-like posture. She felt as useless as a chewed-up core. "I don't know so much. I mean, I *knew* that you should sign on Legacy Day, but you didn't, and nothing I did or said made anything better."

"I like having friends who only tell me the truth," said Raven. "Cedar. Maddie. You. I'm glad you'll tell me you think I royally messed up."

Apple laughed.

"The best part is, even though that's what you think, you still like me," said Raven. "I think that's, as you would say, fairy enchanting. I know we don't agree on some really important stuff, but we both agree that what's happening to Maddie is unfair."

"The unfairest," Apple agreed.

"This is something we can do. Something we *can* make better. But to reach my mother and get her help with the spell, we would have to, I don't know, hack the Mirror Network or something, and I haven't got the faintest idea how to do that. I need your help,

Apple. You're smart, you care about Maddie, and I trust you."

"I…" Hack into mirror prison? Talk to the Greatest Evil Ever After Has Ever After Known? The library suddenly felt freezing. Apple stood up and turned to a window, rubbing her arms with her hands. Outside, on the path to Book End, Apple could just make out Headmaster Grimm, with Maddie slowly, sadly hopping after him. So. Epically. Unfair.

Ever since Legacy Day, Apple hadn't been able to trust her gut. Right now, her gut was telling her to save Maddie. She hoped it was right.

"Okay," Apple said, trying to sound braver than she felt. "Let's do this."

Raven stared at her. "Well, I did not know you were going to say that. A complete surprise. Like, shock of the century, no kidding."

And though she was so scared, her knees trembly and her jaw chittery, overall Apple felt hopeful, full of good, hot energy, as if she'd made the right decision. At last, something she could do. A task fit for a queen.

She grabbed Raven's hand. "Come on. I know just who we need to talk to."

"You realize, Apple, that my mother is locked up in one of those Great Glass Prisons Headmaster Grimm mentioned, and the punishment for meddling—"

"Is banishment, yes," Apple said as they ran out of the library. "But a leader's most important job is to protect her subjects from harm. We need to stand up for those who can't stand up for themselves. And in this case, I'm standing up for destiny, too. Why, besides me, no one's more passionate about following her destiny than the Mad Hatter's daughter! Besides, Headmaster Grimm said it himself—sometimes it's okay to *bend* the rules. Hurry, we have Madeline Hatter's destiny to save."

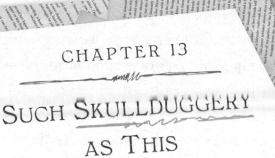

CHAPTER 13

SUCH SKULLDUGGERY
AS THIS

APPLE LED RAVEN TO A DORM ROOM WITH a hand-lettered sign on the door identifying it as the home of DUMP-T STUDIOS. Raven knew Humphrey Dumpty was just the egghead for the hacking job, but she still hesitated outside the door.

"I'll need you to translate the stuff he says," Raven said.

"What, why?" said Apple. "Humphrey doesn't speak a foreign language."

"Not technically, but if you see me looking confused..."

The door was ajar, and they pushed it open wider to find Humphrey Dumpty in front of two table mirrors and a microphone wearing a gigantic pair of headphones over his round head. He turned, and immediately his eggshell-white face cracked a smile. He jumped to his tiny feet, teetering as if he was about to tip over. Raven and Apple put out their hands to steady him before he had a chance to fall and break into pieces. His legs were so thin Raven wondered how they ever held up his body.

"Hey, Humphrey," Apple said, letting go as he found his balance.

"Check, Birdfruit," he said. "What's on the swing?"

Raven looked at Apple with her most sincere "That is exactly what I'm talking about" face.

"Oops," said Humphrey. "I, er...sometimes get, I don't know, *wordspun* when I'm working on, uh, songs and stuff. I mean, hey, Apple; hey, Raven."

"Raven?" Dexter Charming stood up from a couch in the back of the room. He saw Raven and automatically tried to smooth down his brown hair. But as always, a vicious cowlick stuck it straight up in front. He adjusted his black-framed glasses and then put his hands in his pockets, as if trying to look casual. "Oh, hey, Raven, Apple."

"Sorry, I thought Humphrey was alone," said Apple. "We can come back—"

"It's okay," Raven said. "We can trust Dexter. He's cool."

"I am?" said Dexter. He turned away as if he urgently needed to examine a shelf of mirror discs against the wall, but he clearly was just trying to hide a furious smile. Raven didn't think much about it.

"I have another quest for you, Humphrey," said Apple. "Or a re quest, anyway. We need to access a restricted place on the Mirror Network. Um, fairy, *fairy* restricted."

"Whoa. You need the locks taken off the network?" said Humphrey. "I couldn't do that without getting noticed."

"What if you made, you know, a kind of rabbit hole in the network?" Apple said.

"Dig a tunnel, sure," Dexter said, coming closer. "That would get you through without actually blowing the locks."

"Yeah, good idea, Apple!" Humphrey tapped on his MirrorPad and then each of the bigger table mirrors. "Let me just run a test to see if I can do this safely." He tapped a few images on the left mirror, made some gestures on the right, and then spoke into the microphone in a whispered rhyme.

"Okay," Humphrey said. "I've doppelganged—"

"Copied," Apple whispered to Raven.

"—the encryption."

"The locks," Apple whispered.

Humphrey picked up his MirrorPad and gave it a few swipes. "Now I'm doing a test run on my own system doppelganger." He began making gestures on his MirrorPad and occasionally singing at it.

Raven gave Apple a questioning look.

"The oldest, deepest Mirror Network architecture responds better to rhymed voice control than typing or gesturing," said Apple. "Ancient fairytale stuff. You know, 'mirror, mirror on the wall, who's the fairest of them all.'"

"Crown's up, Humph, you've got company," Dexter said.

The two table mirror screens had turned red, and it looked as if faces were forming out of the red smoky image. Humphrey started to chant as he typed rapid-fire commands on his MirrorPad.

> *Check it, D*
> *you're locked in a wee*
> *sea of me*
> *nowhere to go*
> *so fade your glow*
> *and head below*
> *lest I show*
> *my sweet street beat*
> *that I call delete*

The faces faded.

"Whew! That nearly poached us, but I'm in," said Humphrey.

"What *was* that?" Raven asked.

"A mirror daemon," Dexter said. "Sometimes the network locks are there to keep them in, not just to keep us out. But, dude, you *killed* that."

Dexter and Humphrey bumped fists, complete with explosion.

"I must have inadvertently copied one to my local mirror when I doppelganged the security system," said Humphrey. "Let me set up a secure path out of the school's fire-thrall protections from a single terminal, and I'll shunt control to a mirror in your dorm room. How are your rhyming skills?"

"Fairest," said Apple.

"Er, *rarest*," said Raven.

Dexter laughed. "The key is to be threatening and rhyme fast—like you're having a rap battle with the daemon. I'm just okay at it, but Humphrey is the king."

Humphrey shrugged away the compliment but glanced at Apple as if to make sure she'd heard.

"Raven, you should totally lay down some tracks in Humphrey's studio," said Dexter. "Raven's voice is amazing."

"No, it's okay," said Raven.

"You're a singer? Girl, that is *poison*! I'm a music aficionado myself. Here…" Humphrey tapped on his MirrorPhone. Both of the girls' phones buzzed. "I sent you one of my demo tracks."

"Oh," said Raven. "Thanks?"

"Not to groove to," he said, looking shyly down at his foot. "Unless you, I don't know, want to.

But the track I sent is a warding beat. You play it as a loop near the mirror and it'll discourage the daemons."

"That is fairy enchanting," Apple said. "Raven, did I tell you that Humphrey was a talented songsmith?"

She hadn't.

"I think you mentioned it," Raven said. "I mean, that thing you did with the daemon just now could be a song."

"Nah," Humphrey said, cheeks coloring. "The good stuff comes from the soul."

Raven started to edge back to the door. She had a suspicion this conversation was going to turn awkward.

"I have another beat I wrote, Apple," Humphrey said. "It's kind of about you guys."

Uh-oh, Raven thought, *here comes the awkward.*

"It's wicked cool," said Dexter.

"I'd love to hear it," Apple said.

Humphrey turned his crown backward, picked up his microphone, and started a beat from his mirrors.

"Is this a sitting-down thing?" Raven whispered to Apple as Humphrey began to rap.

Yo. Time to light a candle
for change you can't handle, y'all.
Hup!
Down with the standard
gotta get with the band or
try to withstand
the assault of the cult of
the soon-to-be queens
a team of two teens
you'd never expect
Except for the beauty
the two they
share nothing or do they
have more in common than
a blackbird and swan?
This piper, this pawn
tries to stand strong
alongside them
to guide them
but like that Piper I'm pied then
by the twist and the bend of
plot, path, and trend, so
later my friend, 'tis time for
The. End.

Apple squealed and clapped.

Raven applauded rapidly. "Thanks so much, Humphrey. You're a knight in shining eggshell armor. Thanks, Dex. I'm sorry to scat, but we're fairy pressed for time."

"Ain't no thang," said Humphrey. "Raven's standing mirror in your room is programmed with the rabbit hole. Be careful where you browse with it."

"See you later, Raven?" asked Dexter.

"Definitely. Thanks again." Raven grabbed Apple's arm and pulled her out the door.

Raven kept her head down as they hurried through the castle, afraid to see anyone who might slow them down. Maddie had less than twenty-four hours.

Raven shut the door to their room and touched the knob, murmuring a locking spell and squeezing shut her eyes, tensed for the spell to backfire. Her magic always worked better when she used it for evil, but she was never certain what her magic would deem evil. This time, the spell held. Apparently "breaking rules=bad" outweighed "helping Maddie=good." The locking spell wouldn't stop

Blondie—nothing could do that—but hopefully the curly-haired porridge lover wouldn't come around looking for Apple.

Apple was standing in the center of the room, a good fifteen feet back from Raven's ebony-framed, full-length mirror.

"You ready?" Raven asked.

"As ready as I'm going to be," Apple said, staying exactly where she was.

"So as soon as my mirror is connected to mirror prison, remember not to touch it."

"What?" Apple started walking backward. "Wait...you mean there's a chance she could pop out of there and into this room?"

"In all likelihood, it would take a lot more than just touching the mirror to let her out," said Raven. "Headmaster Grimm says the spells binding her in mirror prison are the strongest stuff there is. But my mother is such a powerful sorceress we shouldn't even risk a touch."

"Okay," Apple said, exhaling the word on a trembling breath.

Raven sat on the floor in front of the mirror and tapped it. Instead of merely reflecting her image, icons popped up, opening a connection to the local network. "I can do this alone, if you want. Or at least try to do it."

Apple whimpered quietly but came closer.

"I've only ever contacted my mom from our home mirror," Raven said, "so I'm not sure how to—"

Apple swiped through some commands, and a view of a slowly turning green ring appeared. "This is the data carousel that routes mirror traffic. You can spin the carousel until you get to the path you're looking for."

Raven opened her mouth, closed it, then opened it again. "I have no idea how you did that."

Apple kept swiping the carousel, tapping paths, searching. Raven noticed that its greenish color was bleeding into scarlet.

"Apple!" Raven shouted. A monstrous face was forming—deep eyes, wide nostrils, stubby horns. "We forgot to play the...the...Humphrey loop," Raven said, scrabbling at her handbag for her phone. "The warding beat thing!"

"Of course," Apple said, and in two quick moves, she had her phone out and Humphrey's rhyme was playing.

No fear drear sphere
just a trick o' the mirror
we're a mere fleck of dust
you must adjust
steer clear
veer to the rear
nothing is as it appears

The face started to fade.

"Whew," Apple said. "That was close!"

Raven nodded and crept back to the mirror. "Wait...it's turning red again."

A gargoyle-like face popped back up, opening a huge, toothy mouth.

"Ugh!" Apple said, scrambling again for her phone. With a swipe and a tap, Humphrey's rap was back on. "I forgot to set it on repeat."

Slowly the face, and then the color, drained from the mirror view.

"So can you get us on my castle's network?" said Raven. "There's a mirror there that connects to Mom's prison once a year. If we can find it—"

"Hexcellent idea," Apple said, tapping the mirror.

Raven began to see things that looked familiar.

There was that MirrorChat node for the village kids that her dad was always trying to get her to use, and the place where you could order fried noodles for delivery.

"There it is!" Raven shouted. She slid forward and tapped a dark speck in the corner of the mirror. It enlarged to show another carousel ring with what looked like a single green mirror node. "Whenever I tried to access this on days that weren't approved, this node was dark," she said, tapping it. The words and digital carousel flickered and faded. "Whoa. It's connecting already! Humphrey's hack worked."

Skinny silver sparks buzzed across the mirror's surface. For a moment it was just a mirror, Raven's own face reflected back. Then the view deepened till it seemed she was looking through a window into a sunny, large room with many mirrors on the walls. Raven put her hand on Apple's arm, reminding her not to touch the mirror now.

The Evil Queen walked into view, dark and beautiful. Apple gasped and fell back, scrambling away on her hands.

"Oh!" said the Evil Queen. She smiled slowly.

Each time Raven saw her mother's face, she had the

uncomfortable feeling that she was looking into a mirror—but a *mirror* mirror. They shared the same strong brows, nose, and chin, and the same purple-tinted irises, pale skin. Like her, the queen had purple highlights streaking through her black hair, though usually she also had a little gray. Now the gray hairs were gone. Surely there was no salon in mirror prison where she could dye them, and Raven knew she couldn't have used sorcery to change their color, because the prison blocked all magic.

Usually she wore a striped prison jumpsuit, but now she was dressed in a black-and-scarlet gown as if about to go out to dinner. Or to overthrow a kingdom. Not to mention her cell looked a lot larger than Raven remembered and the walls were covered with mirrors. Perhaps the prison rules had relaxed, privileges for good behavior?

"Raven!" said the queen. "What a pleasant surprise!"

"Uh, hi, Mother," Raven said awkwardly. She had hoped to ready herself before *actually* talking to her mom. Oh well. "It's good to see you, too."

"Of course," the queen said, gesturing dismissively. "But what a surprise to see you in this way. You've broken the locks! But"—she touched the mirror—"you haven't actually broken them. Clever. A little regrettable, but clever." She shifted her position and looked at Apple. "And . . . is that Snow's daughter back there? Participating in such skullduggery as this? Scales and snails, girl, you've surpassed yourself!"

Apple crossed her arms and put on a brave face, but Raven saw that she was shivering.

"I suppose I have *you* to thank, Snowflake," said the queen. "*Years* I've been imprisoned and my own daughter never bothered to sneak in a little extra time with her beloved mother. Not until she befriended the daughter of my nemesis. Well. At least she knows how to make use of her friends."

Raven bowed her head. Facing her mother, she felt six years old again—shy, uncomfortable, anxious that she was doing something wrong. She had to stop that. What she was doing was important, and she needed to be big Raven, Raven who was Maddie's best friend and In Charge of the Situation. Rebel Raven. She took a deep breath and tried to meet her mother's intimidating gaze.

"Well, I suppose it's too much to assume you've come to break me out?" asked the queen.

"Right...no," Raven said. "Sorry."

The queen looked at her nails. "Pity. Just miss me, then?"

"No, I mean, yes, but there's something else."

"I've told you," the queen said, sighing. "I don't know where that wretched stuffed bunny of yours is."

"What? No."

"Stuffed bunny?" whispered Apple.

"I don't know why you held on to that thing for so long," said the queen. "I think it a blessing the nasty little totem found its way to oblivion."

"I found Prince Bun-Bun, Mother," said Raven. "Last year. At the bottom of the moat."

"Great Gorgons, Raven! What were you doing swimming in that filth?"

"Prince Bun-Bun?" whispered Apple.

"I was looking for Prince Bun-Bun," Raven said through clenched teeth. "And I found him."

"Well, good for you. Sometimes one has to do dirty and distasteful things to achieve one's goals," the queen said, looking at her significantly. "Sorry."

Raven was frozen for a moment. *Sorry* was not a word she was used to hearing from her mother. Was she apologizing about the bunny? Or maybe even for all she'd done—not only to Ever After, but to Raven herself? The neglect, the curtness, the years of evil training? Or was she playing games as always? Raven hated this. Still feeling six, she had a sudden urge to run to her father for a hug.

Perhaps Apple noticed, because she stepped forward boldly and put a hand on Raven's shoulder.

"Ms. Queen, we need your help," Apple said.

"Certainly! Just put your hands on the mirror and repeat the words I tell you. I'll be out in a flash to assist you with whatever troubling little dilemma you find yourselves in!"

"Mother, please, we can't do that," Raven said.

"Hmph. I had to try. People are always surprising me with the extent of their stupidity, but no surprises here today. *Yet.*"

"We need your assistance with a translation, Your Majesty," Apple said, fists on her hips.

The Evil Queen snorted and then giggled and then began laughing with such malevolent force and volume that Raven worried the mirror glass would break.

"I'm sorry," the queen said, wiping tears from her eyes. "One doesn't get to laugh much in here, and I found that delightful. Snow White's daughter needs my help! With a translation! Any other homework I can do for you?"

There was a knock at the door. Apple and Raven turned to each other in terror.

"Raven! Apple! Are you ladies okay?" a voice called.

"Quick," Raven said. "Put a blanket over the mirror!"

Apple tossed a blanket as Raven removed the locking spell and opened the door to Professor Momma Bear.

"Hi," Raven said, putting on her most relaxed face.

"I thought I heard something in here," Momma Bear said. "Something...terrible."

"Nope," Raven said. "Just us girls. We were, uh, telling jokes."

Apple approached the door. "What did the zero say to the eight?"

Momma Bear furrowed her brow. "I'm sorry?"

"Nice belt!" Apple said.

Momma Bear and Raven both stared at Apple in silence until Apple gave Raven a significant look.

"Oh!" said Raven. "Nice belt! Ha!"

Apple nodded at Raven, coaxing.

"Ha. *Ha!*" Raven continued to laugh, building volume. "*Mwahahahahahahaha!*"

Apple flinched. Raven had sounded almost exactly like her mother.

"Um," Apple said. "Is that what you heard?"

"I think it was," Momma Bear said, eyes narrowing. "Be careful, girls."

"Okay," Raven said. "Thank you, Professor Momma Bear."

Raven shut the door and leaned against it.

"That was close," said Apple.

"Nice belt?" said Raven.

"You know, because an eight looks like a zero squeezed in at the middle?"

"Oh, okay. That's kind of funny." Raven pulled the blanket off the mirror.

"That," said her mother, "was the height of disrespect." She shuddered. "Now, you need my help. My price is conversation and involvement. I'm bored, and your little problem has a solution just sneaky enough to be interesting."

"Wait, we haven't even told you what's going on," Raven said.

The queen sighed as if exhausted. "Your dearest lunatic friend Maddie is being banished for something she didn't mean to do, and you need to convince that worm Milton Grimm that he's wrong."

Apple and Raven stared.

"How—?" Raven started.

"Since there's no way to force change in Uncle Milty," the queen continued, "well...there is, but I'm thinking you aren't willing to shove a parasitic worm into his brain, correct?"

"Correct," said Raven.

Apple nodded, adding a quiet "*gross.*"

"So. You need to show him and the rest of that petty faculty the whole picture. They need to *see* what happened from every point of view and convince themselves of the truth of the matter. You need Irrefutable Evidence."

"We have this book," Apple said, holding up volume "I."

"Is that Auntie Aesop's ridiculous *Complete Compendium*? Ugh. Not only is she a complete bore, I know from personal experience that she cheats at cards. Anyhoo, I already know the spell, and I'll teach it to you. Then you can drop that truth bomb in

Grimm's face and laugh as he cringes at the realization of his own ignorance!"

"It's not an *actual* bomb, though, is it?" Apple asked.

"No! That's a metaphor, my little fruit bat. Don't they teach you anything in that school?"

"We know what a metaphor is, Mom. We're just making sure."

"Well, yes, there's making sure, and then there's *being a fool*. But, no, it is not an actual bomb. Just a simple revisualization of the event."

"Is it like a reenactment that you can run on a mirror?" Apple asked. "That plays back a view of what was in front of that mirror earlier?"

"Clever little rose hip. If I wasn't boxed in here, I'd pinch your cheek. It's just like that. In the way that mortar and sludge are just like a castle."

Raven sighed. This was typical of her mother: insults hidden in praise.

"She means that a mirror reenactment is similar, but a lot simpler," Raven explained.

"Oh. Okay. This might be a Mirror Networking problem, then," Apple said. "Something for a network reflectioneer to handle, not a sorceress."

The queen's eyes flashed purple, and Raven's mirror actually shook a little.

"*Silence!*" the queen bellowed, pointing at Apple. "And pay attention. You might actually learn to live a life rather than play a Silly! Tedious! Role!"

Apple cringed.

"*Mother!* Enough!" said Raven. "This is my friend! You are doing us a favor, I know. But please try to be civil!"

The fire in the queen's eyes quenched, and she smiled in a way that Raven very rarely saw—a comforting, genuine way.

"There's my girl," the queen whispered.

Raven took an involuntary step back, not sure whether to be glad of or worried by her mother's approval.

"This spell doesn't use actual mirrors," the queen said calmly, as if nothing untoward had happened. "You need the mirrors of the soul, the eyes of those who witnessed the event." She held up a hand. "Before you ask, no, you don't need to remove anyone's actual eyeballs."

Apple and Raven exhaled in relief.

"But you will need specific ingredients to make it

work. Unfortunately, I can't actually tell you what they are."

"What? That's a joke, right?"

"If it had been a joke, it would have been better than that zero-with-a-belt monstrosity. No. The conditions of my imprisonment prevent me from 'casting spells or through my specific words causing spells to be cast.'"

Raven groaned. "Could you at least try?"

"Hat airing," said the queen, "bic spudow, ullrag donks, wise pat, liny agaught, and lastly, a ep." She winced as she spoke, finally bowing her head, fingers pinching the bridge of her nose.

"Was that some kind of Faerie language?" Raven asked.

"No," Apple said. "That's the filter. The mirror encryption enforcing the rules. She probably did tell us the ingredients, but they came through garbled."

"Precisely," the queen said, rubbing between her eyebrows. "And I am punished personally by a demon of a headache for even trying."

"How about a riddle?" Raven said. "Give us riddles for each one, and we'll figure them out on our own."

The queen quirked a half smile. "Perfect. I love this game."

Apple tore a sheet of parchment from her spiral scroll notebook and handed it to Raven.

"Write down the riddles."

"I could just record it on my MirrorPhone and save the parchment?" said Raven.

"That would be a bad idea," Apple and the Evil Queen said at the same time. Apple looked at the mirror, shocked. The queen raised an eyebrow.

"Okay," Raven said. "Why?"

"Because the phone is connected to the Mirror Network," Apple said, pulling her gaze away from the queen. "The stuff on it might be accessible to someone who knows what they're doing. Like Humphrey or Dexter—"

"Or the school administrator—exactly." The queen tilted her head, smiling at Apple and batting her lashes. "Are you sure you're *Snow* White's daughter? Not adopted or anything?"

"Mother!" Raven said.

"Yes. I'm sure," Apple said, pushing a lock of blond hair behind her ear.

"Ugh!" Raven sputtered. "Just give us the riddles, okay?"

"Advice first, or risk the failure of everything you attempt."

Apple scooted closer, notebook and pen ready to take notes.

"In this endeavor you search for truth," the queen said. "This is truth: If you seek help from others, expect to fail."

"So we've already failed," Raven said.

"Because you sought me out?" said her mother. "Don't be a fool, girl. Despite what Milty Grimm says, there are no rules in life. But I am keenly observant, and I notice what happens and which patterns repeat themselves. Take this advice for what it's worth: If you wish to succeed, depend on no one but yourself."

"Okay, but—" Raven started.

The Evil Queen interrupted. "And without question, in no way and by no means let Madeline Hatter know what you are doing. Do this, if not for my sake, for your father's, who would weep unpleasantly over the scraps of his daughter left after a spell gone bad."

Raven stared. "Not tell Maddie? Why?"

"Oh, you know how these things work," said her mother. "Once upon a time, the brave sister must weave seven shirts out of stinging nettles in order to change her brothers back from swans and do it without speaking a word. Blah-blah goody-two-shoe nonsense, but sometimes a spell does require silence, so not a word—spoken, written, even thought—to Madeline Hatter."

"But—" Raven started.

"Got it," said Apple. "The riddles now, please?"

"Very well," the queen said. "I will give you six riddles, one for each ingredient of the spell. The first is this: Willow tree and whispers three…"

CHAPTER 14

BUNNIES! WISP WHISPERING

WILLOW TREE
AND WHISPERS THREE
TOGETHER MAKE A TASTY TEA
IN FORESTS THEY DO GLOW
WHENCE WE DO NOT KNOW
BUT IN THE TEAPOT THEY WILL GO

APPLE READ THE FIRST RIDDLE ALOUD over and over as she and Raven left the school, crossed the Troll Bridge, and entered the Village of Book End. The cobblestone main street was mostly empty, the shop fronts quiet, doors closed, as if the village were in mourning. The news of Maddie's banishment must have already spread.

"Whispers three, whispers three…" Raven muttered. "Glowing in forests…curses, I can't make sense of it. You know who is really good at solving riddles?"

"Maddie," said Apple. "And we can't ask her. How about Kitty Cheshire? She's a Wonderlandian, too. I bet she's royally good at riddles."

"But she's terrible at keeping secrets," said Raven. "How about Lizzie Hearts?"

"Well, your mom said not to ask for help."

"I wish—" Raven started.

"I know," said Apple. "Further proof that Maddie is indispensable! We can't risk asking her, but we should go to the tea shop, anyway. The riddle mentions tea twice. It's our best clue."

"But…but Maddie will be there all day with her dad, and imagine how she'll feel when we can't talk to her."

"Raven, we're doing this for her, and if telling her would break the spell…"

Raven stopped before the red front door of the

Mad Hatter of Wonderland's Haberdashery & Tea Shoppe. She took a deep breath.

"Okay, but this is going to be terrible, because not only can't we talk to Maddie at all... well, we can't even risk *thinking* about the spell while we're with her."

Apple wrinkled her nose. "What?"

"Maddie sometimes hears, um, a voice she calls the Narrator, and that 'Narrator' reports on what people are thinking."

"Wait, we can't think about what we're doing around Maddie because then a *voice* will tell Maddie what we're thinking and the spell will break?"

Apple smiled, expecting Raven to say she was kidding. Raven nodded. Apple lost her smile.

"Clear your thoughts," Raven said.

Apple let her mind go blank and opened the door.

The first thing she noticed was the quiet. Usually the tea shop was full of chatting customers, their conversations like the harmony to the melody of piping teakettles and clinking silverware.

The Mad Hatter was sitting at one of the empty tables. His large, black-and-white-striped top hat in his hands, his thinning mint-green hair exposed.

"No room! We're closed!" he called out.

He was always shouting silly things like that, but this time Apple believed him.

"Oh, it's you, Raven Queen." The Mad Hatter smiled wide around his bucked front teeth. "How is a Raven like a writing desk?"

"Neither is able to feel happy today," said Raven.

The Mad Hatter nodded, and his smile slipped away. "I'm going with her, of course. Closing up shop. Do you think they like tea in Neverland?"

Apple tried to imagine the pirates, mermaids, and Indians in Neverland drinking tea out of dainty cups. Maddie's destiny to become the next Mad Hatter of Wonderland had already been severely compromised when the portal to Wonderland was sealed. At least in Ever After she and her father had been able to continue their destiny by opening the tea shop. But in Neverland...

"We were hoping to get some tea from you just now," said Raven. "Do you know what kind of tea would involve willows and whispers and glowing in forests?"

"Ah, will o' the wisps tea!" said the Mad Hatter. "An exotic brew. Never made any in the shop...

always meant to…" He looked around wistfully at the walls covered in doors, the empty tables set for a teatime that wouldn't come. "I'll just go fetch my copy of *Recipes for Teas, Tales, and Time*."

The Mad Hatter went into the kitchen just as Maddie came out. Apple stiffened. She heard Raven squeak.

"Raven!" Maddie hopped over to them on one foot. "And Apple White. I knew you'd stay with me on my last day. I knew you didn't forget about me after I hopped off."

Raven shook her head but pressed her lips together.

"Sometimes I hop when I'm sad," Maddie explained to Apple. "Because it's hard to stay sad when you're hopping. Your feet bounce your middle and your middle wants to laugh. Try it!"

Apple stood on one leg and hopped. She didn't feel like laughing.

"Raven, are you gloomy and goosey again?" said Maddie. "You don't need to worry about me. I'll be okay. In Neverland. With the—*ah—ah—ACHOO*! Excuse me. With all the pirates and things. I just…I'll miss you so much. When I think about it, I want to…"

Maddie screwed up her face as if fighting off tears. She took a deep breath, bent one leg, and hopped madly around the room. She returned with her smile again in place.

"Hey, why are you girls so quiet?"

Apple cleared her thoughts, focusing on anything other than—no, she wouldn't think it. Instead, she'd think about bunnies. Cute, little, fuzzy bunnies with wiggly noses.

"Apple, why do you keep thinking about bunnies?" Maddie asked.

Apple cleared her thoughts. *Bunnies, bunnies, bunnies . . .*

Maddie giggled. "I love bunnies, too. Are you trying to cheer me up?"

BUNNIES. BUNNIES. THINKING ABOUT BUNNIES. Apple felt a light sweat begin to glisten on her forehead.

"Something strange is going on," Maddie said, squinting through one eye. "Narrator? Why are they acting squirrelly? Like squirrels without hats even?"

Maddie tried to get the Narrator to explain, but the Narrator's job was to observe, not spoil secrets.

"Secrets?" asked Maddie. "What secrets?"

Just what Raven and Apple were…um…Bunnies. So many bunnies.

"Narrator?" said Maddie, shocked. "You too?"

"Here it is!" the Mad Hatter said, returning from the kitchen. "I found the recipe in this book. And I found the book in a hat. And I found the hat in a closet. And I found the closet under the table, though how the closet got under there I'll never know."

Apple read the recipe as quickly as she could. She had to get out of there soon or she would—

BUNNIES. BUNNIES!

Apple handed the book back to Maddie's dad, and she and Raven turned to leave.

"You're leaving?" said Maddie. "You're just going? But…but I…I was hoping—"

Apple didn't look back. *BUNNIES.* She ran outside, Raven following, both breathing heavily as if they'd been holding their breath as well as their thoughts. They kept running down the block till the tea shop was out of sight. Raven sat on the edge of a fountain and covered her face with her hands.

"Did you see Maddie's face?" said Raven. "She thought that I didn't care."

"Let's get this over with fast so you can explain,"

said Apple. "According to the recipe, we're going to need to find will o' the wisps in the Enchanted Forest and make them into tea, which could take hours, and this is just the first item of six. We'd better split up."

Raven nodded. "I agree. We have less than a day to solve all the riddles, collect the items, learn the spell, and use it to defend Maddie."

"Right. So, I'll go chase will o' the wisps?" Apple asked. "And you can tackle the next incomprehensible item on the list."

Apple waved good-bye and ran. Every minute she took crossing the school grounds, the footbridge, and the meadow toward the Enchanted Forest was one minute less in the day. She tried not to think about the Kingdom Management quiz the day after tomorrow, or that paper due in Damsels-In-Distressing, or that work sheet for Experimental Fairy Math she was supposed to be doing, or—

Maddie. Right now, Maddie is more important than protecting perfect grades. A good ruler thinks first of her own subjects. Uh, people subjects, not school subjects. Hocus focus, Apple!

The moment she crossed under the canopy and into the shadows of the Enchanted Forest, a white fluffy streak slammed into her chest, knocking her to the ground.

"Gala!" said Apple. "I missed you, too."

In all the drama after Legacy Day and then Yester Day, she hadn't taken time to come visit her pet in the Enchanted Forest. The snow fox nuzzled into Apple's neck and then ran a circuit from atop her head down her arm, up the other arm and over her head again several times, finally stopping to perch on Apple's knee. Apple looked into Gala's shiny black eyes.

"Gala, sweetie, I'm trying to find a will o' the wisp. Can you help?"

Gala reached forward to touch her cold black nose to Apple's, then she launched herself off Apple's knee and began to run. Apple followed her loping white shape deeper and deeper into the forest. The shadows were so dark they gleamed purple.

Purple, like her *eyes* ... Apple thought, shuddering.

The Evil Queen made Apple nervous, but that was only natural—after all, that's how the Snow White story went. Then again, she hadn't been quite as scary as she'd imagined. She was just Raven's mother, right? She was helping them, wasn't she? Besides, as evil as she was, the Evil Queen was still an elder with a lot of knowledge and experience, and Apple thought it wise to learn what she could. From the Greatest Evil There Ever Was. As she went about on her errands. Collecting spell ingredients.

Apple gulped. And hoped she was on the right path after all. But how could she know for sure when everything had gone so totally off script?

The only surety, the only safety at all, was in following her destiny. And Apple would do everything she could to protect not only her own destiny but also everyone else's—including Maddie's.

Up ahead was a clearing with a grand gray willow tree at each end. From afar Apple could see a glowing sphere about the size of a baseball bobbing above the ground on a breeze. Suddenly it disappeared. Apple had spotted these will o' the wisps in the past, but until reading that passage in the Mad Hatter's recipe book, she hadn't understood what they were.

Faerie is a realm alongside our own, invisible to most. Only its residents—fairies, pixies, sprites, and such— move freely between it and Ever After. Sometimes, on full moon nights or right after a rainfall, one may catch a breath of Faerie flowers, their rich scents passing briefly into our world. Besides Faerie's residents and the occasional aromas, another traveler from There to Here are the will o' the wisps.

One of Faerie's most beautiful flowers is the enchanting dandyrose. At the end of a dandyrose's life, it erupts into a puff of downy white seeds called will o' the wisps. They are so light they sometimes catch a breeze in our world and cross over, especially near willow trees. They disappear and reappear as they move back and forth between Faerie and Ever After. Will o' the wisps glow in the nonmagical light of our realm. They follow whispers, and so serve as an interesting ball in the pixie game of Wisp Whispering.

Not until Apple stood on the edge of the clearing could she hear the whispers.

Tiny pixies flew around the field, some guarding the goal zones by each willow tree, others surrounding the glowing ball, whispering madly at it. Half wore blue jerseys, half green, both sides tackling each other, trying to keep members of the opposite team away from the ball.

When the will o' the wisp disappeared, the two

pixies on the sidelines began screeching words Apple didn't understand. Both teams of pixies spread out over the field, forming a grid pattern. A few moments passed, and the pixies waited, spinning in place, watching. When the ball winked back into existence farther down the field, the nearest pixies swooped to it, tackling one another and whispering at the ball to *follow, follow.*

Apple tiptoed up to the two pixies who were hovering off to the side—one in blue, one in green—who she assumed were the coaches.

"Pardon me," Apple said softly. "I'm sorry to interrupt your fascinating game, but I need a favor, please."

One of the pixies flew by her ear, buzzed loudly, and flitted away. The other made a noise Apple would swear was laughter.

"Um, I really need a will o' the wisp—it's to help a friend?"

The pixies were screeching at the players, completely ignoring Apple now.

"Can you help me, please?" Apple asked.

The pixies glanced at her and returned their attention to the game.

Boys and woodland creatures were quick to help Apple White, but the pixies were unaffected by her genetic damsel-in-distress trait. Perhaps they didn't speak her language.

Apple knew someone who surely spoke theirs.

"Gala, sweetie, do you think you could find Ashlynn Ella?" Apple asked.

As soon as her snow fox was out of sight, Apple began to have doubts. The Evil Queen said they must do this alone. But here she was asking Ashlynn for help. And for that matter, the Mad Hatter had helped, too. Had she already damaged the spell?

Then again, what did "don't ask for help" really mean? Was Raven supposed to get all the ingredients herself? Or was Apple? She could feel herself spiraling into a series of questions that she wouldn't be able to answer. This was exactly why things needed to remain on script.

She's evil, Apple reminded herself. *You can listen to what she suggests but don't have to do exactly what she says.*

Apple did not have long to fret. Ashlynn was already returning with Gala. Her long strawberry blond hair was loose but for a braid encircling her head like a headband. She wore mint and coral, her presence bringing a bouquet of bright colors into the forest shadows.

"Wow, that was fast!" said Apple.

"I was nearby waiting for...*someone*..." Ashlynn cleared her throat. "Gala said you needed my help?"

"Yes, I need to make will o' the wisps tea for...*something*..." Apple also cleared her throat. Apparently, they both had secrets. "And I was wondering—"

"Pixies!" said Ashlynn.

One of the pixie coaches yodeled, and the two teams flew off the court and straight to Ashlynn, buzzing around her, tidying her hair, giving her tiny kisses on the tip of her nose and ears. Ashlynn giggled. They jabbered in high voices Apple couldn't understand any more than she could understand the buzz of a honeybee, but Ashlynn had no trouble.

"It's so good to see you all, too. Who's winning today? Really? Wouldn't that give the blue team three straight wins? I see, how fascinating. Yes, I'm sure the green team has an excellent chance. I see you recruited two new whisperers. Oh my, now don't tell me that, you know my fondness for moths. Yes, of course I'll let you get back to the game, I was just wondering, do you have a spare wisp my dear friend Apple could have?"

There was indeed a spare wisp wandering just out of bounds behind a willow tree. Several pixies from both teams whispered it over to Apple. She thanked them and held the glowing thing in her hands. It tickled her palm like a static-electric feather. Before it could disappear, Apple removed a gold ring from her pinkie and threaded some of the wisp through it. The Mad Hatter's book had said only metal would ground the wisp in Ever After until it could be brewed.

The pixies returned to their game, and Ashlynn watched them for a few moments, cheering moves Apple didn't quite catch.

"I should go," said Ashlynn. "I have to, uh, meet that *someone*."

"Thanks, Ashlynn!"

Apple had just left behind the shadow of the forest when another shadow cast her in shade. She looked up to see an elephant-sized dragon.

"Nevermore!" said Apple. "What a pleasant surprise. Will you go find Raven? She could probably use some help."

The dragon snorted and flew off.

Apple felt the will o' the wisp vibrate in her hand, as if it had caught a breeze in Faerie and would have passed over if not for the little gold ring anchoring it in Ever After. Apple began to run. She needed to get that wisp into a teapot and tackle the next riddle.

This was going to be a long day. But, for Maddie's sake, would it be long enough?

CHAPTER 15

MADDIE C~~HATS WITH~~ 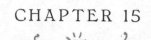 Sneezes All Over
THE NARRATOR

M ADDIE SAT ALONE IN THE TEA SHOP kitchen, feeding tiny pieces of cheese to her dormouse, Earl Grey. It was unclear if she could hear the Narrator or not.

Of course I can, Narrator. I am mad, after all.

Okay, I…uh, I'm not supposed to talk to you, you know, but I just feel so bad about what's happening, especially with—

Achoo!

Bless you. Don't tell me you have a cold on top of everything else?

No, it's just that they're sending me to Neverland, and you know how pirates...ah...ah... Achoo! Pirates make me sneeze. I'm pretty sure I developed an allergy to them on Yester Day. Now even the thought of—Achoo!—of pirates makes me sniffly and itchy and prone to bursts of air exploding out my nostrils.

Oh dear. There are a lot of pirates in Neverland.

Yeah...I'll get used to them eventually, right? I am sorry that my dad is losing his tea shop. And most of all about leaving my best friend till The End Raven Queen...but she's too busy to spend my last day together, so maybe she doesn't really mind that I'm going away.

Oh, Maddie, I wish I could share with you everything I know.

I wish I could share with you some of this lovely charm blossom tea paired with raspberry preserves on a warm baguette. You know, baguette almost rhymes with p-p-pir—Achoo!

CHAPTER 16

BLESSED BEAST OF TERROR

THE CROWN OF TERROR PAST
THE SHELL INSIDE STILL LASTS
THE ITEM YOU SEEK, A TOY OF THE WEAK
MAJESTY DOWNED, RUN AGROUND IN TOWN
TO ECHO NOW NAUGHT BUT HAPPY SOUNDS

RAVEN WALKED ALL OVER BOOK END. The riddle said, "run aground in town," and in that she hoped it was literal. Book End was the only town around. She snooped through narrow alleys where so little sunlight filtered between the roofs that the fairy streetlamps stayed on all day. She jogged through residential areas with town houses fit so tightly together they resembled books on a shelf. She stalked open streets lined with pumpkin houses, giant shoe houses, and crooked houses at the end of crooked paths. And all the while Raven repeated the riddle to herself, but nothing caught her eye.

The only place she didn't wander was Book End's Main Street, where the Mad Hatter's Haberdashery & Tea Shoppe sat mostly empty and totally sad. Raven couldn't bear to see Maddie again and not say, or think, a word.

Usually she and Maddie would hang out together on a weekend like today, chatting over late breakfast and tea and then going shopping or heading to the Enchanted Forest and hanging with Nevermore and picking flowers and other ingredients for teas.

And now, she just didn't know. Maybe she *was* evil after all, if doing what she thought was right only ended up making people suffer.

No, she thought stubbornly. This *wasn't* her fault. All she had wanted was to choose her own life, her own destiny. Raven sighed. She couldn't be blamed for everything getting out of control, right? Was it her fault that people saw what she did and—

Never mind! Solve the cursed riddle for Maddie. She needs you now.

What the hex was a "crown of terror past"? An actual crown? No. Crowns were never really crowns in riddles. They were always hats, or kings or queens, or things that sit on top of stuff.

Raven heard laughter echoing down an alley. Little kid laughter. That counted as "happy sounds," so she followed it to the playground.

She found a bench and sat. It was one of those candy benches that had become popular in parks a few years back. Raven remembered that her dad let her eat an entire peppermint armrest from a park bench near their castle. This one was old, though. All the good bits had been eaten off or were now so calcified that you'd break your teeth if you tried. She adjusted, and her skirt stuck a bit.

The playground had the standard castle play set, with a candy-cane climbing pole that everyone licked on the way down. Raven was amazed now that she'd never gotten sick doing that, or sprained her tongue or something. There were a giant boot playhouse, a slide that looked like a tongue lolling out of an ogre's head, a small merry-go-round spinning all around a mulberry bush, a mini glass tower kids could save one another from (or save themselves, as Raven used to when she was little).

In the center was a huge climbing dome, only this one wasn't a spiderweb shape like normal, it was molded to look like the skull of a dragon. She walked up to the play skull and touched it. She'd lived with her mother long enough to be able to recognize the feel of actual bone. This skull was the real deal.

Raven laughed out loud, and a couple of parents nearby eyed her warily. She ignored them and did a little happy dance.

"That's the Evil Queen's daughter," she heard someone whisper.

Let them whisper all they wanted. She'd solved the riddle! The "crown" was the head, the "terror" was the dragon, the "shell" the skull. And the children were using it as a "toy." But Raven's giddy feeling turned into a cringe when she took a step back and realized it would take a team of horses to pull it free. Besides, how could she get it up to her room unseen? Let alone fit it through the door. She needed help, and that was exactly what her mother had said she shouldn't have.

Just then Nevermore flapped down on her leathery wings and landed next to her. Even though she was in her more polite large-dog-size, parents scattered, screaming.

"The Evil Queen's daughter!" someone yelled. "And her evil dragon minion!"

"Woofie," came a small, excited voice from somewhere near her knee. A tiny girl, probably no older than two, had toddled up to Nevermore. She had her hand out, and Nevermore nuzzled it. "Woofie," the girl said again, giggling.

"Azure!" called a voice.

Cedar Wood came running up. She was smiling, the wood of her face supple and full of movement. Her face and arms were a warm brown and showed the delicate curves of wood grain, and her dark brown hair was full of wavy curls. She wore her casual day-off clothes—lederhosen overall shorts with a paint-splattered T-shirt beneath.

"Hi, Raven!" said Cedar.

"Hey, Cedar," said Raven.

"How funny. When I heard all the screaming,

I actually thought, 'I wonder if Raven's nearby.'"
Cedar's smile recarved itself into mortification.
"Sorry! Not that you're always making people scream
in terror or anything...though you do sometimes, I
can't tell a lie. Um, shutting up."

"Woofie," said the little girl.

"Who's this?" Raven asked.

"Little Boy Blue's daughter. Sorry if she's mauling
Nevermore. She's kind of obsessed with dragons."
Cedar took Azure's hand. "Everything that's happening with Maddie really huffs and puffs, you
know? If I had a stomach, I'd be sick to it. I'm going
to go over to her shop this afternoon as soon as I'm
done babysitting Azure and help them pack. Will
you be there?"

Raven shook her head. She was afraid if she talked
about Maddie, she'd cry. Cedar must have noticed,
because she gave her a hug.

"I know you, Raven Queen," she said, pulling back
to look at her. "And I know that if you aren't with
Maddie today it's because you're trying to figure out
a way to save her."

Raven pressed her lips together.

"It's okay. You don't have to say a word," said Cedar.

"I know spells sometimes require secrets—especially from someone like me who can't help blabbing!"

"Cedar, can I ask you something? Is all this, all the bad stuff happening with Maddie and everyone angry and the food fight and the Treasury—is it my fault? Because I didn't sign the book?"

Cedar frowned. She was cursed to always tell the truth, and Raven feared whatever she'd say next wasn't something Raven wanted to hear. Cedar opened her mouth.

"Never mind," Raven said quickly, suddenly desperate to change the subject. "So, um, you're creative."

"What?" Cedar asked, tugging Azure away from one of the pokier parts of Nevermore.

"You're a painter and artist, so you, like, think outside the dungeon. Can I talk something through with you?"

"Sure," Cedar said. "Is it okay if," she finished, pointing to Azure, who had climbed her way up to Nevermore's back and was waving her arms.

"Fwy, Woofie! Fwy!" she shouted.

"Oh, that's totally fine," Raven said to Cedar, and then, to Nevermore, "Um, *don't* fly."

The dragon huffed and sat, curling her tail around herself like a cat.

"So I have this really big thing that I need to move from the village to my dorm room, but people can't really know about it. Any ideas?"

Cedar looked at her out of the corner of her eye. "This has nothing to do with Maddie and some spell to save her, right? Right. I'm not asking. So how big is it?"

"Like." Raven looked around, trying to find something as big as the dragon skull that wasn't actually the dragon skull. She gave up. "As big as that play set there."

"That is big. Well, okay, I'm just going to start saying stuff out loud. It's how I work with my art. Try stuff out till I find something that works. Um, you could take it apart."

Raven opened her mouth to say how that wasn't possible, but Cedar just kept going.

"And take it in piece by piece and reassemble it. You could disguise it as a giant and roll it in on wheels, you could hire a giant to carry it, you could magic zap it into a marshmallow and carry it there. You could, um, shoot it out of a catapult, turn it into a flying machine, have Nevermore carry it for you, find a hidden relic that stops time and use it to stop time and then take your time to move it in whatever way you wanted, pour a Shrinking Potion on it (and then an Embiggen Potion after you move it), teleport it, dig a wishing well under it, talk to it and see if it will walk there on its own..."

"That's good!" Raven blurted, holding up her hands to stop Cedar at the same moment that Azure toppled off Nevermore. The little girl landed directly in Raven's arms, giggling.

"Enough dragon tumbling for you," Cedar said, taking the little girl from Raven. "Is that good? I can do more—"

"That was plenty," Raven said. "Thank you."

"No problem," Cedar said. "Maybe I'll see you at the shop later? And if not, I know whatever you're doing for Maddie, you're doing all you can."

Cedar carried Azure off to the vine swings, while the little girl called, "Woofie, Woofie!"

"Well, 'Woofie,'" Raven said to the dragon, "did anything Cedar say—"

Raven was interrupted by the sounds of screaming. Nevermore had transformed into her full, terrifying size, crushing the bench she was perched on.

"Nevermore!" Raven shouted.

The dragon popped back to small size, and instantly everyone stopped screaming.

"Cedar suggested you could carry it," Raven said. "When you're big, you'd be strong enough to pull it out, but there's still the problem of how to get it through the normal-sized window of my normal-sized room."

The dragon enlarged again, the nearby crowd picking up its scream right where it left it. Her suddenly huge wings knocked Raven over. Nevermore helped her up with the nudge of a horned nostril, and then instantly shrank down. Everyone stopped screaming.

Again, Nevermore popped big. The crowd screamed. Nevermore shrank small. The crowd sucked in a gaspy breath, preparing for the next scream.

Raven giggled. "That's just mean. You're scaring them out of their minds."

She gave her pet dragon a tight hug, hoping to

keep her from popping huge again, but also because she just needed a hug right then. "Just stay small for now, okay?"

Nevermore chuffed a puff of warm air into Raven's neck. Raven pulled back and looked into Nevermore's eyes.

"Were you trying to tell me something with all that small and then big stuff?" Her dragon just stared at her. Raven really wished she could speak dragon. "We need to shrink that skull, don't we? Just like Cedar said. Except we don't have a Shrinking Potion. Or an Embiggen one."

Raven had the magic within her to do the size changing, but a spell backfiring in a playground might accidentally turn a child into a toad, or a toad into a child. Raven's mind spun and finally stopped on a thought.

"You're a dragon, and that skull is made of the same stuff you are," Raven said. "Do you think if you shrank yourself while holding onto the skull, *you* could be the Shrinking Potion?"

Nevermore huffed again and took to the air, as large as an elephant—an iridescent black, scaly, leather-winged, and dagger-clawed elephant. Such an airborne monstrosity would fuel the nightmares of all the townspeople for weeks. They screamed, of course. The dragon landed on the skull and in a twinkle shrank to a more manageable size. And so had the skull.

Raven jumped in the air. "You did it! You blessed beast of terror you!"

Nevermore dipped low in the air, careening to one side, the shrunken skull in her talons. Her wings beat furiously and she stopped before crashing into the ground.

"Do you think you can fly it back to my room?"

The dragon bobbed her head and was off. Raven watched her soar away and felt her shoulders relax.

"Um, excuse me?" she heard a small voice behind her say. She turned to find a little boy in short purple pants and a puffy hat. "Why did that dragon steal our jungle gym?"

Children were edging toward the big, empty hole where the skull had been.

"Oh," Raven said. She hadn't thought through the whole stealing-from-little-kids part. Her mother would be so proud.

"I'll have her bring it back," said Raven. "I just need to borrow it for a bit."

"Will the dragon come back, too?" the boy asked, eyes big as a kitten's.

"Woofie!" Azure struggled out of Cedar's arms and came running back. When no dragon appeared, her nose sniffled like a bunny's and then the tears came.

"Do you think Azure could play with Nevermore?" Cedar asked. "It would make her day."

Raven brightened. "Oh! Yes, that would be totally wicked! It might be kind of amazing for her, too, you know, getting to play with kids who actually want her around. It's not easy when everyone thinks you're evil all the time when you really mean no harm and don't want to hurt—"

Raven stopped, embarrassed Cedar might think she was talking about herself.

Cedar smiled. "I think the screaming was mostly parents. The kids thought she was fairy cool. Except for the part where she took their jungle gym, of course."

"Woofie!" Azure shouted, insistent.

"Right, I'll hurry," said Raven. "Um, better stand back."

Raven had wasted too much time already solving her first riddle. The sun had passed its zenith and was sliding down into afternoon. It would take forever to walk back to her dorm.

Besides, if she did something spectacular, maybe the kids would think she was cooler than she was scary, like Nevermore. Time to risk a little spell.

She whispered the words, pointed at her own feet, and let the magical energy zip down her arms and out her fingers.

She was airborne before she realized it had worked. Sort of. She'd been hoping for a temporary flight spell. But, nope, she'd catapulted herself.

Raven would have screamed if she'd been able to suck a breath from the fierce wind rushing at her face. She shot out of Book End, zooming over the Troll Bridge. Ahead, the Ever After High castle was looming larger and larger. There was the open door on her dorm room balcony. And around it, a whole lot of hard, unforgiving wall.

Raven cursed herself for trying to show off. Fitting that she would end like a bug smashed on a hybrid carriage windshield.

CHAPTER 17

FAIRY BALL
of Certain Death

BIG TO THE SMALL
IT GROWS ON ALL
SMALL TO THE BIG
ONE THREAD OF A WIG
UNWANTED AND PLUCKED
IT DROPS IN THE MUCK

THE BEANSTALK WAS A COLOR OF GREEN that made Apple wish for sunglasses: so green it almost sparkled. And so alive it never stopped growing. She could actually see the stem (thick as a hundred tree trunks) slowly twisting, the enormous, broad leaves almost imperceptibly lengthening from the stem, uncurling themselves, and turning toward the sun. A kind of whispery noise emanated from it, the sounds of growth, but it seemed to Apple that the Beanstalk was quietly singing to itself.

"One thread of a wig..." Apple repeated to herself. It had to be a hair. A big hair. The hair of a giant. And the surest place to find a giant was at the top of the Beanstalk.

Apple gulped. She'd climbed Jack's Beanstalk before with Briar. But, still, even wearing the climbing harness she'd borrowed from Briar's dorm room, that was one intimidating vegetable.

Only when she was near enough to touch the lower leaves did Apple notice the makeshift barricade surrounding the Beanstalk's base. Two ogres sat in folding chairs in the shade of a tent-sized leaf, quietly munching from bags that read:

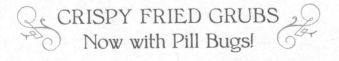

CRISPY FRIED GRUBS
Now with Pill Bugs!

Apple started to pull back one of the barricades.

"Nope," said one of the ogres.

"Yep," said the other ogre. "Nope."

"I'm sorry?" Apple asked, confused.

Both ogres began to stumble over themselves in an attempt to explain.

"They gotta thing up there…"

"There's this stuff…"

"Jumpin' and sum other…"

"But it's a list you got…"

"Enough!" said a third voice.

Apple looked for the source of the voice. A bright green sprite stood on a Beanstalk leaf perfectly camouflaged. Her hair, wings, and stylish motorcycle boots were all the same color of green.

"Well, hello!" Apple began.

"I'll stop you right there." The sprite hovered directly in front of Apple's face. Her eyes were glowing green. "Don't try any flattertalk. Just go away."

"Ah, c'mon, Amy," one of the ogres grumbled. "Why you gotta be so mean?"

"*You!*" the sprite shouted, darting straight to the ogre. "*Shut it!*"

The ogre bowed his head.

Apple took a breath. "Hello, Amy, is it? My name is Apple White. Would you be so kind as to tell me why the Beanstalk is closed?"

"Sporting event up there." Amy hefted the tiny MirrorPad in her hand. "And you're not on the list. There are rules, you know."

Apple groaned. She respected rules. Rules existed to keep everything going in the right order, on track, safely and securely, with as little uncertainty as possible. But here rules were stopping her from trying to get everything back on track.

Apple's mind raced. She'd read a book two years ago during King's Break, *The Dust Trade During the Age of Djinn*, detailing the historical economics of trade between magical creatures. Briar had made fun. "A book about dust? That has got to be the driest tale ever!"

There had been a chapter on how the court of the sprite regent only traded in ideas, thoughts, or feelings, which made doing business with them awkward and confusing. Instead of a load of potatoes, they would trade something like "the satisfaction of a full wagon," or instead of a diamond they would trade "a bride's beauty."

Well, it was worth a shot.

"It is a pleasure to exchange thoughts with you today, Amy," Apple said in what she hoped was the formal sprite manner.

The sprite's little eyebrows raised in surprise. Her lips cracked a tiny smile, revealing green teeth. "And with you, Apple," she said.

Apple clasped her hands together. She was on the right track.

"I am thinking today…" Apple said, gazing up at the clouds that swallowed the top of the Beanstalk. She needed to express her need to get up the Beanstalk and into the giants' castle, but in the sprite manner. "…about transit, and passage, and entry."

Amy smiled and flitted back to the leaf she had been sitting on when Apple arrived.

"Ah," said Amy. "My thoughts bend toward duty, gates, and…" Her eyes flicked to her ogre companions "…frustration."

"Perhaps we could trade?" said Apple.

"What do you offer?" she said.

"I would take your frustration in exchange for passage," Apple said.

The sprite sighed and turned away. Whoops.

Apple messed up there somewhere. What she wanted was to somehow make this sprite's life easier in exchange for the chance to go up the Beanstalk.

"But I fear it would be a poor exchange," Apple said, trying to recover.

The sprite nodded.

"I am feeling free, Amy," Apple said. "Right now, I am feeling like I could take a break. Alone, away from large distractions, maybe to have a cupcake. I want to trade my freedom to you, Amy. You mentioned duty before. Your duty. I'll take that in trade. You can relax, and I think duty suits me."

The sprite brightened. She flitted up to Apple's cheek and patted it. "Deal. Let us also trade gratitude."

Apple laughed in relief and happiness. "Agreed," she said, and watched Amy fly off toward town. Probably to the cupcake shop. Hopefully she and the pastry vendors could work something out, because Apple was pretty sure they wouldn't take something like "duty" or "frustration" as payment.

With the sprite gone, a quick, friendly conversation with the ogres delegated the door-guarding portion of her newly gained duty to them, and she proceeded to the Beanstalk base. Ogres, Apple found, were often reasonable when treated kindly. A climbing rope was wrapped around it, and Apple clicked a hook onto the first link and began the long, arm-aching, stomach-trembling, dizzying climb.

"I. Don't. Like. Big. Weeds," Apple breathed, wiping her hands, sticky with bean sap, on her skirt.

At last she breached the cloud cover and climbed up into noise. Masses of people and creatures sat in towering bleachers, blocking her passage to Giant Castle. And no giants in sight.

A huge banner hung over the cloud field:

🐍 EVER AFTER HEXTREME! 🐍
HeXtreme Games, Second Edition

Apple looked around, desperate to find some way around the crowd and to the castle.

A witch in black spandex and a pointy black hat was floating on a mop about ten feet above the crowd. She was standing straight up, holding the mop vertically, with one boot on the floppy business end of the mop, one hand holding the pole part. A massive mirror broadcast her image to the crowd.

The witch shouted into a megaphone. *"Next event: Fairy Ballll...Ballll...Ballll!"*

The crowd cheered, and four teams of two people ran onto the cloud field, each in matching bright outfits.

Apple heard a voice she recognized.

"What do you mean, he doesn't meet the height requirement?" Briar yelled. She was wearing a bright pink minijumpsuit and sporty wedge sneakers, her dark brown hair swept up in a ponytail. As always, crownglasses were perched on her head—a sleek, aerodynamic pair today.

"Rules," said a plump, bearded man with a bird on his shoulder.

Apple moved closer and nearly tripped on Nate Nutcracker.

"Whoa," she said, stumbling. "Sorry, Nate! I didn't see you there."

"Story of my life," Nate said, smiling to show he didn't mind, though his forehead was worried. He was also wearing a bright pink minijumpsuit.

"Wait...you were going to compete with Briar, and they won't let you because—"

"Stature," said Nate, his tiny hands shaking.

"That's not fair," Apple said, her fists going to her hips. "And if there's anything I don't like, it's unfairness."

"No, it's totally okay," Nate said. His nutcracker jaw was chattering. "I'm actually re...re...relieved."

Still, Apple marched up to Briar, ready to give the referee a piece of her mind.

Briar stopped her yelled protests midsentence. "There!" she said, pointing at Apple. "There's my new partner!"

"Wait...what?" said Apple.

Briar grabbed Apple's hand, tugging her onto the field. "I had no idea you wanted to start doing hextreme sports, Apple!"

Apple skipped erratically behind Briar, trying to keep up without tripping. "I, um, I don't. Actually, I just came up hunting for a giant's hair."

"Really? Gross."

"Yeah," Apple agreed.

"Stand here," Briar said, pointing to a small circle combed into the cloud field. "Fairy Ball is a cool event. You'll be okay. Hey, I'm throwing a going-away party for Maddie tonight in my dorm. You must be there, of course. I know we all want to cry our eyeballs out about it, but crying makes for lousy partying, so tonight we dance and sing and just spellebrate the wildest, maddest girl in all of Ever After."

"*Release the balls!*" shouted the announcer-witch.

Apple looked around. She had been hoping that Fairy Ball was some kind of ballroom dance-off, but there was no music, and everyone seemed to be looking...up.

Apple looked up just in time to see a giant, silver, spherical blob plop heavily onto her and Briar. She felt slimy for a second, and then, *pop!*, she was inside the sphere, looking out onto the world through a shimmering haze.

"Wait..." said Apple. "I'm here for—"

"A giant's hair, I know," said Briar. "Don't worry, I can help."

"But—"

"*Go!*" the announcer yelled.

"*Run!*" Briar screamed.

"*Aah!*" said Apple.

But she ran.

As Briar and Apple ran, the ball began to roll. It surrounded them like a rubbery cocoon, powered by the motion of their tread. Apple watched through the transparent curves as the other balls passed them.

"Is ... it ... a race?" Apple asked, panting.

"Yeah!" shouted Briar.

The ball was surprisingly bouncy beneath her feet, like running on a trampoline. She laughed. "Why is it ... called a Fairy Ball?"

Briar pointed to either side of them. "Because of the wings!"

Tiny gossamer wings were attached to the outside of the ball. Only they weren't spinning with the ball, just flapping once every time their ball seemed to make a complete rotation. Apple imagined that if the ball were spinning fast enough, it might actually fly.

"Faster!" Briar shouted.

Apple tried to pick up the pace, but she kept slipping on the unfamiliar surface. Three Fairy Balls cruised along in front of them. She hoped that Briar wouldn't feel bad about losing.

Suddenly the Fairy Ball in first place disappeared. It just dropped out of view.

"Briar?" she asked.

"Faster!" Briar shouted, laughing.

The second ball dropped out of sight.

"Briar? Why are there wings on the ball?"

The third one disappeared, and then Apple saw it. They were running right off the edge of the clouds.

"So we can fly!" Briar yelled, and their Fairy Ball rolled off the edge and fell.

They both began to scream, though Briar's scream was "*Hextreeeeeeeeme!*" and Apple's was more of an "*Aaaaaaaaaahhhhhhh!*"

Apple could see the other competitors now, their Fairy Balls spinning, tiny wings flapping, bobbing in the air as if they were floating in water. She would have found it pretty had she not been nearly incapacitated by terror.

"But I needed to go," said Apple. "To. The. Giant! Castle!"

"I know," said Briar. "I can help!"

They sailed past the ball that had been in third place, the second, and then the first.

Apple stopped screaming. "Hey! We're winning!" Briar and Apple gave each other a high five, and then looked down. The ground was coming up remarkably fast. They weren't "winning" so much as falling faster than anyone else. Apple looked at Briar with wide eyes.

"*Faster!*" they both screamed.

Apple scanned the ground below. They were dropping too fast, and they were going to go *splat*. It was all wide stone ground and cobblestone streets. They needed to land in water or hay or something softer than a hammer.

"What's that?" Apple asked, pointing to a large gray mass.

"The. Giants'. Midden. Heap," Briar said, panting with the effort of running.

The midden heap. The giants' garbage pile. Gross. But way softer than stone. And just maybe...

"Do the giants throw their garbage and stuff there?"

"Yep!" said Briar. "Maybe even the hairs after a haircut. But... it'll be nasty."

Apple shrugged, as much as anyone can when running for her life.

Briar looked at the oncoming rush of ground. "*Let's do it!*" she yelled, sprinting.

The Fairy Ball containing Apple White and Briar Beauty crashed into the giants' garbage heap with a sound like ten thousand butter pies exploding. The ball burst on impact, its remains lying like a gelatin picnic blanket under the girls. For two seconds they sat in silence, stunned that they were not road paste.

Briar broke the silence. "That. Was. *Awesome!* Let's do it again!"

Apple took a breath, thought better of it, and then began absently patting herself to make sure she wasn't missing any arms or legs.

"Um," she noised, standing unsteadily. "I can't. Have an errand. To run."

The word *run* reminded her how she'd just run for her life, and she shuddered.

Briar hopped up. "What do you need the hair for anyway? Hextra credit project? Never mind, I don't want to know any gross details." Briar tore a couple of pieces off the ball's remains. "Here, we can use this to board down the heap so we don't have to ruin our shoes in this nastiness."

"Thanks, Briar. I'll see you back at school."

Her friend gave her a thumbs-up and leaped onto her impromptu garbage surfboard. "Wahooo!" she yelled, sliding away.

Apple looked around the garbage heap. Huge orange peels, banana peels, crumpled tissues, and (*shudder*) sharp toenail clippings. Snow White had to face an Evil Queen, creepy forest, poison apple, and glass coffin, but at least in her story she'd been safe from giant midden heaps.

At last she spotted a thin, stiff stick as long as her arm poking out from under a monstrous, wilted cabbage leaf. A giant hair. She didn't have enough time to climb back up the Beanstalk and try to find the giants all over again. Besides, the riddle did say "drops in the muck." Maybe the most garbagey hair was exactly what the spell needed.

"Be brave," Apple told herself.

She teetered across a path of garbage, moved aside the leaf, and pulled out the giant's hair. It was black and rough to the touch, like the bark of an oak tree. Holding the hair firmly, she sat on the scrap of the gelatinous ball and slid down the heap. After falling from the sky, sledding over garbage was a walk in the park.

CHAPTER 18

THE OPPOSITE OF QUIET!

SEEK THE SPAWN OF THE PAWN
OF THE CRONE OF BONES
THAT COTTAGE OF DOOM
THE ROOM NOT A ROOM
THE BEAST NOT A BEAST
THAT MOVES SOUTH AND WEST AND NORTH AND EAST
SEARCH IN NEST, COOP, OR DEN
OF THE COBBLED TRUSSED HEN

RAVEN WAS CATAPULTING THROUGH THE AIR.

I'm going to die now, Raven thought. *I'm going*

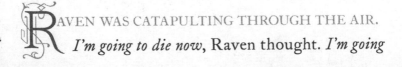

to smash against the side of the castle like that spoonful of porridge against Apple's cheek.

Beyond the breathless terror and dizzy delirium, she noticed that the sun was lingering over the horizon. Only a couple of more hours of daylight.

Maddie…

Raven refused to die. She shook her head to focus her thoughts, fought the air to point her hands toward her feet, and tried a spell she'd never attempted before. Streams of high-powered fire shot from her hands. Her speed increased, rocketing her through the cool air, but she could move her hands and control her angle at least. She wiggled her hands, adjusting her trajectory, aiming for the open door on her dorm balcony.

She hurtled through it and crashed in a heap on Apple's bed. The remnant of her fire-hands spell spurted out, but not before setting afire one of Apple's throw pillows. It had been her favorite, too—Briar had ironed on a photo of the five boys from the band One Reflection. Their smiling faces scorched and turned into ash. Raven whimpered. Apple would not be happy. They were really cute boys.

Raven quickly swept off the ash and straightened

the satin bedspread. Apple always kept her things tidy.

Nevermore was perched proudly atop the shrunken dragon skull, flapping her wings and squawking like a chicken.

"Good girl!" said Raven. "Could you go back to the park? I kind of promised the kids you'd play with them. Come back at sunset, okay? Or before that if people show up with torches and pitchforks." Always good advice.

She gave Nevermore a good-bye neck scratch and then unfolded the parchment from her pocket.

"'Seek the spawn of the pawn...'"

She read the next riddle over and over again, pacing. The sun was lowering still. "'...the beast not a beast...'" *No time, no time.* "'...search in nest, coop, or den...'" *Maddie. Save Maddie.* Her panicked heart scattered her thoughts. She needed to calm down and refocus.

Raven gave up on pacing and sat at her vanity, opening it to reveal a hidden keyboard.

It was a Legacy Day gift from her father. He didn't know yet that she hadn't signed, only that she hadn't been excited about it. But he had known the most perfect gift possible. Raven sat, letting her fingers roll out a melody that was both haunting and sweet, a tune that whispered a new day was full of possibilities, risks, fears, and joy. She didn't have to be evil. She didn't have to take after her mother. The past couple of days she'd been feeling afraid of the unknown hole uprooting her destiny had left inside of her. The music reminded her that while freedom was a little frightening, it was also beautiful.

She had claimed her own destiny. There was power in choice. And she would use the power to help save Maddie.

Raven began to sing the riddle into the melody. "'The crone of bones...that cottage of doom...the room not a room...'"

She stopped and laughed.

"I've got it!"

She laughed so hard she put a hand over her mouth and tensed for the sound of Professor Momma Bear's knock. It didn't come.

Raven ran out to the balcony and scanned the courtyard below.

Every day at sunset Baba Yaga's hut dropped the witch off at the dungeons. Whatever Baba Yaga did down there had to be done in the dark of night, and, frankly, Raven didn't really want to know what it was. She was more concerned with the Hut.

A "cottage of doom," both a "beast" and a "room." One of Madam Yaga's titles was "Bone Witch," and that was about as close to "Crone of Bones" as you could get. She needed to track the Hut to where it "slept" at night. Its den or nest, as the riddle said. Whatever she needed would be there.

With a heavy flapping of wings, Nevermore dropped from the darkening sky to land on the balcony beside Raven. The dragon had a ribbon tied around one horn and what looked like princess pea-butter smeared above one eye. Raven wiped off the smear.

"Did you have fun playing with the kids, girl?"

Nevermore cocked her head in a noncommittal gesture. Raven smiled. At least she didn't get hurt by any overprotective parents, and...Raven examined the dragon's teeth, claws, and other pointy bits. No blood, so nobody else was hurt, either.

"I'm going on another treasure hunt," Raven said, scratching the dragon along her spine. "Want to come?"

The dragon hopped up like an excited dog, and Raven laughed. "I guess that means yes. First, we need to watch for Baba Yaga's hut—hey!" She turned just in time to see the Hut walking on its giant chicken legs away from the dungeon entrance. She'd almost missed it! "That! I need to follow that!"

Nevermore took to the air and popped into her large size. Raven hurriedly shoved on her Coat of Infinite Darkness, climbed on the balcony railing, and jumped. When she landed on Nevermore's back, the dragon dipped down a bit. Even full-sized, she wasn't a grown dragon, and carrying Raven was an exertion, especially after she was tired out from hauling the shrunken skull and playing with children. Raven patted her neck, grateful.

The evening air was cool, the remains of sunlight making the sky a golden gray. Nevermore swooped down around the castle and spotted the Hut just as it leaped over the ravine and started across the meadow toward the Enchanted Forest.

Nevermore dove as if for an impact attack.

"We can't catch it, sweetie." Raven leaned forward to speak into Nevermore's ear. "We have to be quiet. Just follow it." The dragon let out a screech of understanding, and Raven winced. That was the opposite of quiet.

The Hut's two front windows looked around warily, and then it hopped into the Enchanted Forest.

"Okay," Raven whispered, and the dragon gently lowered her to the ground.

Raven ran to the forest's edge. Under the canopy, the forest was too dark to see. Raven risked a small spell, producing a pale purple light from her fingertip. She spotted the large chicken foot tracks and followed.

She stopped. In a small clearing the Hut waited, blinds open, windows staring in her direction. Raven held her breath, but from behind she heard the loud *slap-clack* of her pet dragon's clawed feet as she ran toward her. The Hut tensed, and when Nevermore crashed into the clearing, the Hut bolted. The dragon started to give chase, but Raven leaped on her tail.

"Wait!" she said, dragging along. "We can't chase it! We have to just follow it. Quietly!"

Nevermore looked back at her, confused. Raven groaned. This wasn't going to work.

"Okay, girl, I'm going to need you to scout for me. Fly over the forest. Look for the chicken house."

The dragon poised to leap into the air, but Raven put a hand on her muzzle. "But stay in the air. Just stay above it. That way I'll know where to go, okay?"

The dragon bobbed her head and took to the sky. Raven watched as Nevermore flew back and forth over the forest, stopping, circling, and then moving on. Eventually, she hovered in one place. Raven ran into the darkness.

She tried to go as straight as she could in the direction that Nevermore had shown, but she ended up darting around and back and forward, over a rabbit warren and under dangling sprite nests, gleaming as silver as new coins in the thin shafts of moonlight. After a few minutes she was completely lost.

Cerise would be better at this. She could dart through this forest with no trouble and probably sniff out the Hut. But the Evil Queen had said to work alone.

The forest canopy was too thick here to find Nevermore. Raven sidled up to a tree and looked for a branch to grab. She had never been much of a tree climber. It had always seemed sort of creepy to climb all over something that was alive. She sighed and leaped to grab the lowest branch. She caught it and swung to pull herself up, but the branch snapped with a loud crack.

The tree screamed. Raven scrambled back from where she had fallen. She'd never heard a tree scream before, but this was the Enchanted Forest, after all.

"I'm sorry, I'm sorry, I'm sorry," she whispered, wincing for the thing to uproot itself and eat her.

It didn't, but the scream did come again, and this time she realized it wasn't the tree, it was something behind the tree, and farther away. When she heard a grunt she recognized as Nevermore, she ran toward the sound. She stumbled several times, finally crashing down into a broad, treeless gully. Nevermore was hopping back and forth like a puppy waiting to chase a ball and facing a very angry Hut.

The Hut scratched deep furrows into the ground with its chicken claws and let out another one of those screams that Raven had thought was a tree in pain. Nevermore darted forward and nipped the Hut on one of its eaves. The Hut growled, stomped its feet, and charged. The dragon let out a happy screech and scrambled into the forest, the Hut in angry pursuit.

Which left Raven alone, except for the egg.

The egg! There was a giant nest in the center of the

clearing made of branches, mud, and a few hextbooks. And in the center of the nest was an egg. "Seek the spawn," the riddle had said. The offspring of Baba Yaga's cottage. And there it was, a dotted oblong egg nearly as big as Raven was. She ran to the nest and tried to lift it, without success. She pushed, and it rolled. She shoved, and it slid. All she had managed to do was shift the egg's position in the nest.

That scream again, in the trees off to her left.

Raven scrambled away from the egg, out of the nest and into the shadows of the forest just as the Hut returned. It sniffed around with its front door opening and closing rapidly, its blinds all the way open. It sat on the nest protectively. Raven's Coat of Infinite Darkness helped her blend with the shadows, but it couldn't completely hide her from the cottage's notice.

Nevermore returned. The Hut chased it away. But as soon as Raven crept back into the nest, the Hut smelled or heard or sensed her somehow and returned to sit on its egg.

This happened over and over again until Raven spotted the moon rising high above the canopy.

Maddie, Maddie, no time, no time . . .

She walked around to find Nevermore.

"One more favor?" she whispered.

Several minutes later Nevermore landed. Cerise Hood was clinging to the dragon's neck spikes, her white-streaked dark hair wild, her hood down, her wolf ears up. Her eyes were wide, her mouth frozen in a grimace.

"Cerise," Raven whispered, waving her arms so that Cerise could spot her despite the magical camouflaging of her Coat of Infinite Darkness. Cerise's gaze landed on her, and she blinked in surprise.

"Riding a dragon is kind of fun, isn't it?" said Raven.

"I think I prefer my own two feet," Cerise said through her grimace.

"I could really use those feet," said Raven. "And the rest of you as well."

Raven explained the situation.

"So you need me to steal the egg of Baba Yaga's monstrous cottage but can't tell me why?"

Raven nodded.

"But you swear it's for a really, really, really good reason?"

Raven nodded again.

"Um...okay," said Cerise.

"Okay?" said Raven. "You mean, you just believe me?"

Cerise put a hand on her hip. "Raven, it doesn't take a genius to put this together. Whatever you're doing, you're trying to help someone else, because that's the kind of thing you do. And that someone is obviously Maddie, and you can't tell me because spells are involved somehow and spells often require secrets or silence, and so I won't ask. But I trust you."

Raven nodded. She felt a little sniffy, any reply stuck with the emotions in her throat.

This time, when Nevermore led the Hut away, Cerise put up her hood and vanished, not camouflaging with the background as Raven's coat allowed her to do but actually traveling through the shadows. Cerise was swift and invisible in the darkness, only a moment later appearing in the nest. She bent her knees, lifted the egg with both arms, leaped out of the nest, and ran.

Good godmothers, but that girl was strong.

Raven ran, too, following Cerise away from the nest. Another scream. The Hut was following. Cerise was strong and darted through shadow to shadow, but the heavy egg was slowing her down. If they couldn't outrun the Hut, they'd end up on the wrong end of a giant chicken foot.

They were stealing. That was evil, right? Maybe dark magic would work.

"Wait," said Raven, catching up to put her hands on the egg.

"Hover, float, levitate," she whispered.

Her hands began to glow purple, but nothing happened. She started to hear crashing sounds in the forest. The Hut was getting closer.

"Balloon, fluff, glide," she said.

The light around her hands flickered and went out. The ground was shaking beneath Raven.

"Hurry," Cerise said.

Raven slapped her hands on the egg. "*Up!*" she yelled. There was a bright purple flash, and the egg went up. Fast, like a launched cannonball. It flew into the sky, and Raven's stomach dropped. It was going to fall. It was going to crack, the spell would fail, and Maddie would be lost forever.

Raven and Cerise watched the egg sail up, up, up, and into the claws of Nevermore, who swooped away with it.

"Yes!" Raven cried, and started to clap until she felt the light from the windows of a very angry cottage hit her. She stopped, turning slowly. The Hut was standing five feet from her, staring. She still had her Coat of Infinite Darkness on and felt herself trying to dissolve further into it. Cerise, hood up, had already melted into a shadow. Raven stayed frozen. She waited for what felt like twenty minutes, and then finally the Hut backed itself into the nest, and its windows darkened. Raven waited one more minute to be safe, and then slowly crept out of the forest.

She started the run back to the castle. She was one item closer to performing the spell and saving Maddie.

CHAPTER 19

THE BUZZ OF A SPELL

APPLE TRUDGED THROUGH THE DOOR OF their dorm room, dropped something long and stick-like on the floor, edged around the dragon skull, and flopped onto her bed.

Raven looked up from the riddle parchment. "You look less, er, radiant than usual."

"I met up with Briar, again," Apple said, her voice muffled from the pillow her face was pressed against. "I fell from a tremendous height into a pile of giant garbage. It was a long walk back from the Beanstalk. A bunch of songbirds tried to help me. You know how sweet they are, but it took, like, a hundred of them to lift me up, and, honestly, we traveled about as fast as I could walk, so...wait, where's my One Reflection pillow?"

"Um...is that a giant hair?" Raven said quickly.

"Mmm-hmm," Apple said.

"That makes sense," Raven said. "Big to the small, plucked, wig, right. Good thinking."

Apple turned her face from the pillow. "Is that a dragon's skull?"

"Yup," Raven said. "Crown of terror past."

Apple sat up. "Did you...slay it?"

Raven let out a giggle before she could stop it. "No. It's old. Kids were playing on it in the park in town."

"You stole a toy from children? You *are* evil," she said, with a tone of mock horror.

"Stop," Raven said, smiling. "I let them ride Nevermore in trade. I'm not sure she's forgiven me."

"Is that a huge egg?"

"Yep, the spawn of Baba Yaga's chicken-legged cottage. And I see you brewed some will o' the wisps tea."

"Though it's surely cold now. We'll have to heat it

up when we need it," Apple said, sitting up. "Okay, enough rest. What are you working on?"

Raven held up the parchment and read aloud.

> THE STONIEST OF GREENS
> PLAGUE QUEENS NOT YET QUEENS
> JUST ONE BENEATH CAN STEAL THE SLEEP
> OF MAIDENS COUNTING SHEEP

"I have no idea what 'stoniest of greens' means," Raven said. "It's driving me crazy."

Apple thought for a moment. "Oh! I know this one!" she said, and reached under her mattress. "A-ha! I thought I felt one under there." She pulled out a pea and handed it to Raven. "A pea. Only the best for princesses' mattresses."

"Of course!" Raven gasped. "I've been trying to figure this out for like an hour, and you just walk in and get it. Duh. A pea. Well, good."

"We do have one more," Apple said, pulling out her parchment.

> A TOOL USED BY FEW, INDEED JUST ONE
> WHOSE SONG THIS WAY IS SUNG:

Barbs Flung
Hearts Stung
Bells Rung

"What could that be?" Apple asked.

Raven reached behind the couch and held up a pink archer's bow. "Cupid's bow," she said.

"You have it!" Apple said. "How did you get it?"

"Um...I asked Cupid if I could borrow it, and she said yes," Raven said.

"Enchanting! Let's save Maddie!"

They smiled at each other. Then looked around at the spell ingredients.

"Um...what do we do with these?" asked Apple.

"I'm going to have to talk to my mom again," said Raven.

Raven performed another locking spell on their door and took the blanket off the mirror.

Apple pulled her chair up to the mirror. "I'll start Humphrey's loop."

Raven sat beside her. "I'll do this alone, if you want."

"Not on your destiny. I want Maddie saved, too. I'm staying."

They made the connection to the Evil Queen, who immediately looked at Apple and said, "You're not staying."

Apple, indignant, crossed her arms. "Yes, I am. I'm here to help."

"Sitting there like a shiftless albino mouse does not count as helpful," the queen said. "Are you a witch, a sorceress, a medium, or possessed of any totems of incredible power? No? Then go away. You will only distract us."

"But—" Apple began.

Knock knock knock.

Raven startled, looking at her door.

"Apple? Apple, are you in there?" came Briar's voice.

Raven turned to her mother and held a finger to her lips. The Evil Queen rolled her eyes.

"You haven't been answering my hexts. Come on, the party already started." Briar's voice turned away as if talking to someone behind her. "Glitter poop, I don't know where they are."

Raven tensed. If Briar was talking to Blondie, then it was all over. One touch and that door would open to Goldilocks's daughter.

But then Briar said, "Sorry, Maddie, I don't know what's going on. It doesn't seem like either of them to forget about your farewell party."

"I saw them earlier ... they didn't talk to ..." Maddie stopped as if choking up. And then Raven heard the sound of Maddie hopping away.

Raven exhaled and met eyes with Apple. Apple reached over and squeezed Raven's hand. Raven nodded but still felt gutted.

"Oh, gag me with a wand," said the queen. "Enough sentiment, let's get back to kicking Apple White out. Now, my little puppy, you will go to the Treasury. That's where the spell must be cast, and things there need to be as close to the order they were in before your unfortunate riot as possible."

"You want me to clean the Treasury?" Apple asked.

"I want you to put it in *order*. I suspect you have a talent, or at least a tendency, for such things. One is put in mind of a certain untidy house full of chaotic dwarves, after all. The spell works best if the physical circumstances are exactly as they were at the beginning of the event. If they're drastically different, the spell might not work at all."

"Well, I'm not a hundred percent sure how the Treasury was, but I could try—"

"Then go, tartlet! Leave. Us."

Apple left at a brisk pace, her chin lifted regally.

"Mother, I've asked you not to be rude to Apple," said Raven.

"Telling lessers what to do isn't rude. They crave leadership."

"Not that it matters, but, technically, Apple is royalty and not your lesser."

"Please. Did you see her outfit? What is she, Miss Cheery Twinkle Toes? She should take a page from your book. *You* look nice. Would it hurt her to wear a little black, for ogre's sake? All that white and gold and red hurts *me*. Honestly, just looking at her blazing outfits gives me a sunburn."

"Mother…"

Her mother grinned. "I can't wait to see your story play out. You are far superior to that little chicken. You're going to rule that story with *her* as Snow White."

"I'm not—"

"Oh, that's right, you're not going to become the next Evil Queen." The queen frowned, somehow looking even more beautiful than when she smiled. "I worry about you, Raven. What will you do now?"

"Save Maddie."

"No, I mean after that. For your life."

Raven sucked in a breath. There was that raw, empty place inside her, the hole where her undesired destiny used to grow. "I... I don't know."

"My advice: If you ever have the chance to change the world, don't hesitate. Leave your great big mark. Let no one doubt that Raven Queen marched through this life in her own way, and let nothing stop her from getting what she wanted."

Raven had been considering just curling up under a blanket for a few years, but her mother's words flickered in her, like the buzz of a spell just before it's cast. What could she do with her life now that it was hers?

"Um... we should work on the spell," said Raven.

"Right. Gather the ingredients. Let me see if you're a fraction as clever as I hope you are."

CHAPTER 20

SMILE LIKE YOU ☺ MEAN IT ☺

THERE WERE NO MORE WINDOWS IN THE Treasury, but the great gaping hole in the wall let in dawn's light. The songbirds began singing, almost as if they didn't know it was just a few hours till Maddie was magically banished from Ever After forever after.

And the Treasury was still a disaster. Frankly, despite an entire night of Apple's best woodland-creature-assisted cleaning, the Treasury resembled Beauty Palace on a rainy day. When Briar's eight little brothers were all trapped indoors, well, no room was safe.

Apple wiped her brow, paused sweeping, and said aloud, "I can't get it done by myself."

But the Evil Queen told them they must do it alone. To trust no one. To lean on their strengths alone.

"Wait…she's evil," Apple said to a squirrel, who was sweeping up wall debris with its fluffy tail. "She's, like, honestly *evil*-evil. What if she's wrong— or even just lied?"

Squeak, said the squirrel.

During Snow White's story, her mother had somehow survived sharing a castle with the Greatest Evil the World Has Ever Known and come out of it not only okay but Happily Ever After. What advice would her mother give?

Apple knew because Snow White had cross-stitched the words on a pillow and propped it up in the informal receiving room: WHEN LIFE IS ALL DARK WOODS AND POISONED APPLES, REMEMBER YOU HAVE FRIENDS. Snow White had stitched messages on other pillows, too, such as: SQUIRRELS WILL NEVER LET YOU DOWN, UNLESS THEY'RE HIBERNATING; THERE ARE ALWAYS BIRDS; NATURE LOVES A BROOM; LOVE IS KNOWING A RABBIT NEEDS YOU; HUGS ARE HOW IT'S DONE; DOUBLE HUGS FOR THE GRUMPY; TREES AND

DOGS ARE HAPPY, SO START BARKING; and others. Honestly, it was hard to find a sofa in the enormous White Castle that didn't sport a cross-stitched pillow. But the REMEMBER YOU HAVE FRIENDS one offered the most insight to Apple at the moment.

Apple ran to Blondie's room and knocked. Blondie opened the door, rubbing her eyes. She was wearing fluffy bear slippers with a blue nightgown, her hair in curlers. When she saw Apple, she put a hand to her hair.

"It's naturally curly, I swear," Blondie said. "The curlers are just for…for…taming the, uh…"

"Blondie, I need your help," said Apple. "You have everyone's MirrorPhone credentials for your Mirrorcast show, right? Can you send out a private message to all the students who were in the Treasury that day—everyone except Maddie—and ask them to meet me there now?"

The Evil Queen may have suggested they not ask others for help, but she most definitely had warned that telling Maddie would nullify the spell. Apple wouldn't risk breaking that rule.

She hurried back to the Treasury. Bright yellow caution tape that read BEWARE! BEWARE! BEWARE!

crisscrossed the door. But the door itself was broken, its lock having been smashed by a swing of the jabberwock's tail, and Apple easily opened it. Apparently, with the Uni Cairn gone and the wall broken, the headmaster wasn't as worried about keeping the Treasury locked up tight.

Within minutes the small crowd gathered, looking through the threshold as if afraid to go in. After all, jabberwockies might be lurking.

"Dear friends," said Apple. "Raven and I are trying to save Maddie from banishment, but we need your help. We're working on an Irrefutable Evidence spell. It will show the faculty what really happened here that evening, and if Maddie didn't break the unicorn-prison-thingy, then she'll be free."

"What if she did?" Blondie asked.

"Well...but what if she didn't?" Apple said.

The crowd shifted. No one entered the room. Apple cleared her throat.

"Um, in order for the spell to work, the Treasury needs to be as close as possible to how it was before the riot. So I need your help. To clean it up. And fix it. Please."

Everyone looked around: the monster-sized hole

in the wall, broken wall stones littering the floor, bashed pedestals, shattered glass display cases, treasures lying around, a giant helmet fallen from its gigantic suit of armor. The floor was swept, but fixing all that was broken seemed insurmountable.

"Yeah, good luck with all this," Sparrow said, turning to go.

"We have to try!" said Apple. "Please, for Maddie, we have to try."

Sparrow paused. The crowd shifted but still seemed unsure. Apple bit her lip, searching for something, anything to do. Her mind clung to the advice her mother had given her.

Smile, Apple. Smile like you mean it.

Could her mother have meant more than Apple thought? Maybe this group just needed to believe there was a chance of success. People would work for something once there was a hope it would work out.

So I have to believe first, Apple thought.

"We can do this," Apple said, smiling. "We can do this," she said, smiling bigger. And the longer she smiled, the more she believed it. "Look at all the talent in this room! Why, there's almost nothing we can't do when we work together."

Now not only her smile felt confident, but Apple did, too, from the tiara she'd pinned in her hair sometime yesterday down to her white ballet flats with gold thread trim.

And then Apple thought of Old King Cole, and she laughed. Some of the students looked startled, but Briar smiled and said, "What? What's funny?"

"Everything!" said Apple. "I mean, isn't it? Kind of funny? What were we thinking, storming into the Treasury where things like jabberwocky prisons are kept? Well, we made a mess of things, but that doesn't mean we can't have fun while we fix it!"

"I'm always up for fun," said Briar.

"Briar, you enchanting girl you," said Apple.

"Yes, Apple, you fabulous slice of pie?" said Briar.

"I think we need to rock this thing."

Briar put her hand on her hip. "I know you're not suggesting that I party-up this dismal scene, because you know I'll do it all the way."

"All the way, Briar Beauty," said Apple. "All the way."

They bumped fists.

"Oh, hey, Melody Piper would be a great help for you, I think," Apple said.

Briar got to work. Under her supervision, Ginger

contributed some freshly made finger foods, and Melody Piper brought in her turntables and started the music. Briar got some people chanting parts of the songs, and good energy flowed through the room.

But much of the crowd just shuffled around the Treasury, unsure, perhaps, where and how to start fixing things.

Make eye contact, Apple's mother had said, but surely she had been talking about more than good manners. *Look back, and look deeper.*

At first glance, Blondie was a talkative, bubbly girl with really great curls. But as Apple looked closer, she noticed earnestness, an eagerness to be involved...and under her arm, her ever-present MirrorPad.

"Blondie, did you happen to film anything that happened that evening in the Treasury?" Apple asked.

"I did!" Blondie said, lifting up her MirrorPad. "You know, in case something newsworthy happened I could use in my Mirrorcast. But just at the beginning, before I got distracted by all the crowns."

"The beginning is perfect!" said Apple. "You have a valuable record of how the Treasury looked. You will be in charge of returning the misplaced items where they should go."

Blondie's eyes brightened. "Yes! Thank you! I will help make everything just right."

"Cerise and Duchess, we'll need supplies," said Apple. "You're so good at Basketball in Grimmnastics, Cerise, I bet you could be quick to gather materials in your basket. And in swan form, Duchess, you're such a fast flier. Will you two work together getting the builders what they need?"

Duchess looked at Cerise out of the corner of her eye without deigning to turn toward her. She sniffed as if smelling something foul.

"We could make it a race," Cerise said. "You know, just to keep things *interesting*."

Duchess's lips curled into a smile.

"I could fix this wall if I had some grout," Hunter called out.

Cerise smiled, too. There was a flash of red as Cerise ran and a puff of white as Duchess changed into a swan and took to the air, off to fetch grout for Hunter.

The wall looked like a big job, even for someone as skilled at making things as Hunter was. Besides, the pairing of Duchess and Cerise was giving Apple an idea. And Briar with Melody, too. Royal working with Rebel...

"Oh, Lizzie!" Apple called.

"Off with her head," Lizzie Hearts said automatically, though she didn't seem to mean it.

"Lizzie, I've seen you build the most amazing house of cards from your deck. And a bridge, too. It was truly inspiring."

Lizzie sniffed and kept looking just over Apple's head, as if making eye contact were beneath her.

"What I mean to say is, I think you're fairy, fairy talented."

Lizzie blinked rapidly and peeked at Apple. "Really?"

Apple nodded, holding that eye contact and smiling confidently. "I really do. I've always thought so."

Lizzie smiled, too, and for a moment she didn't look like a haughty, royal queen—she looked like the young girl she was beneath the Heart crown and behind the flamingo scepter. Apple began to suspect that the seemingly aloof daughter of the villainous Queen of Hearts actually had a tender heart.

"I was wondering," Apple asked, "can you make more than houses and bridges of cards?"

Lizzie leaned forward and whispered, "I can make *anything*."

"I suspected as much." Apple took Lizzie's arm and walked her to where Hunter was working. "How about a wall?"

Lizzie pulled a deck of cards from her purse and shuffled them so they flipped through the air, arcing in the shape of a heart.

"Hunter, you're royally talented at fixing things," said Apple. "Can you and Lizzie work together to remake the wall and window again?"

"It would be my pleasure. A Huntsman is ever ready to save the day." Hunter put his fists on his hips, striking a pose. Out of nowhere, trumpets played a fanfare. Apple startled. No matter how many times she witnessed the Huntsman-To-the-Rescue Move, those trumpets always caught her off guard.

"I knew I could count on you!" said Apple. "Oh, Cedar, could you clean up the glass from the broken display cases? I think anyone else might risk getting cut."

"Being made of wood has its advantages!" Cedar said.

"Cupid, you always have good advice. Know of a way to mend broken glass?"

Cupid fluttered over to Apple, landing between her and Cedar. Apple noticed she wore her quiver of heart-tipped arrows but not her bow. Raven had that, hopefully perfecting the Irrefutable Evidence spell with her mother.

"My arrows mend broken hearts when I manage to shoot straight, which I rarely do," said Cupid. "Little-known fact: I can't hit the broad side of a palace."

"That must be awkward, given your destiny."

Cupid shrugged, her countenance as rosy as her pink hair. "It's okay. I've found people would rather have good, solid love advice than an arrow shot through their heart anyway. But my arrow tips are handy for mending things besides hearts. If I could get someone to hold the glass bits together for me..."

Her gaze drifted over to Dexter.

"Dexter!" said Apple. "I need a prince to come to the rescue of Cedar and Cupid."

"Of course!" said Dexter. "I'm happy to help any damsel, or anyone really. I'll do what I can. Um...where's Raven, by the way? Just wondering."

"Raven will be here soon," said Apple. "Hey, Kitty, we need to get that helmet back onto the giant suit of armor. If you held on to it and disappeared, reappearing up on the shoulders of the armor, would the helmet go with you?"

"Maybe..." Kitty Cheshire said. She made a low, purring noise. "But *fixing* things isn't really my thing, oh Fairest One of All."

"Would you do it for Maddie?"

Kitty wrinkled her nose like a cat offered a bath. But she nodded. "For Maddie."

"Daring, can you help Kitty?" Apple asked.

"I think I'm better suited to something more dangerous and heroic." Daring straightened his crown.

Apple looked at Daring and looked closer. Explaining the why of it all again wasn't going to change his mind. Logic did not motivate her future Prince Charming. So Apple tilted her head, batted her eyelashes, and said, "Please?"

Daring bowed. "Well! Of course, my future queen. Anything for you." Daring began to examine the helmet. "I shall require a rope to tie the helmet to the suit!"

"Um..." Apple looked around. "Holly, could you help out?"

Holly hefted her hundred feet of hair. "Of course! Rule three in our Princessology hextbook says a princess is always helpful. But rule fourteen says a princess must be dignified at all times. Do you think using my hair as a rope is dignified?"

She gazed hopefully at Apple.

"Don't worry, I believe being helpful *is* dignified," Apple said.

Holly breathed out in relief. "Oh good. It'll take me a few minutes to braid a strand, and then I'll cut it out."

"Oh!" said Apple. "Cutting a lock out of your fablelous hair! Are you sure?"

"It grows back fast, trust me," said Holly. "Besides, anything for Maddie. I dreamed about Ever After High for years! I want everything to stay as magical as the first moment I arrived. And it won't be, not even close, if Maddie isn't here anymore."

"We can't afford any interruptions if we're going to get this done on time," said Apple. "Ashlynn, can you ask some of your wee friends to keep watch and warn us if any faculty member is coming?"

"Of course!" said Ashlynn. "I know a very nice family of mice living in the wall near here, ooh, and just the sweetest little cricket...." Ashlynn wandered off with a far-off expression, shouting, "Oh, mousey!"

"Apple," said Blondie, "one of the seven-league boots slid under Charon's boat, and I can't reach it."

"Hmm...we need a tool, or else someone small. Hopper, can you lend a flipper?" Apple asked.

"I can't just change at will, you know," said Hopper, straightening his bow tie.

Apple studied him a moment—looking deeper, as her mother had advised—and caught him casting a furtive glance at Briar.

"Oh, Briar!" said Apple. "Could you help us out for a minute?"

Briar left Melody to run over, because Briar rarely walked if she could run instead.

"What's up?"

"Could you tell Hopper here how dashing he looks today?"

"I...uh...hi, Briar...um..." Hopper stuttered.

Briar looked him up and down. "Hmm, that is a risky fashion choice wearing shorts with a brocaded blazer, but I must say, Hopper, you pull it off. You even look kinda cute."

Hopper blushed red, then green, then plopped down to the floor in frog form.

"Squeeze your charming, little self under that

boat, Hopper, if you'd be so kind," said Apple, "and fetch the boot?"

Briar's party atmosphere had kept Sparrow and his Merry Men around—though they were just lounging against the wall, eating pies and singing along to the songs.

"Oh, Sparrow!" said Apple, smiling sweetly.

"Don't bother asking," said Sparrow. "We don't do floors."

"Or windows," said one of the Merry Men.

"Right, or windows."

"Do you do thievery?" Apple asked. "Headmaster Grimm took the heirlooms you and Maddie stuffed in your pockets and locked them in his office as evidence. I wonder if you could manage to steal them back. Of course, breaking into his office might be more than you can handle...."

Sparrow stood up straighter. "Nothing is more than I can handle. But be careful what you ask for, Apple White." He put a hand on her back and dipped her low, smiling that bad-boy smile. "Or next I might steal your heart."

He winked at her and ran off. Apple rolled her eyes but put her smile back in place.

It was working! Maybe her mother had been right. Apple *could* help fill the world with sunshine, even if things were broken now. After all, sometimes it was the cracks that let the light in.

They only had the few hours till Maddie's scheduled banishment at midmorning, and Apple kept herself busy, answering questions, hiding glass slippers and cobbler's shoes so Ashlynn wouldn't get distracted, batting her eyelashes when necessary to keep Daring motivated. But the sun kept rising outside the rapidly shrinking wall hole.

Apple needed to fetch the headmaster, Maddie, and the faculty before they went to the wishing well for the banishment spell. But she didn't dare leave. She couldn't risk this group dissolving into another riot.

Helga and Gus Crumb were wandering around the Treasury as if lost in a vast forest, wearing embroidered green clothes, knee-high socks, and hiking shoes.

"Helga, Gus, tell me," Apple said, watching their faces closely, "don't you think Headmaster Grimm is royally perfect?"

Their eyes widened slightly at the sound of his name as if in pure adoration. Apple nodded, satisfied.

"I suspected that you support Headmaster Grimm

and his plan to return this school to normal. In order to keep things as they were, we need to protect everyone's destiny, including Madeline Hatter's. Can I trust you to go fetch him, Maddie, and the faculty and bring them here?"

"Vhat do you tink, my cousin Gus? Should ve do vhat de fruit girl asks?" said Helga.

"*Ja*, vhy not, my cousin Helga? If she promises a treat."

Both looked at Apple with wide, expectant eyes.

"Sure, I can find some candy for you if you—"

They ran off.

Apple was expecting the Crumb cousins to take fifteen minutes at least to track down the headmaster's group and bring them all back, but she underestimated the motivation of candy. Just a minute later Ashlynn came running in.

"Apple, the mice say the headmaster, Maddie, and several others are coming up the stairs."

"No, I thought we had a few more minutes," said Apple. "The room isn't finished yet, and we're out of time!"

"I can help with that." Darling Charming, Daring's little sister and Dexter's twin, entered the room. She wore a pale blue-and-purple gown with black lace trim, and for some reason her clothes were shinier than Apple remembered. Darling smiled shyly behind a hand fan. "I want to help Maddie, too. She is so funny! So I can give you a little more time by slowing it down. Please avert your eyes for just a few seconds."

They all turned their backs or covered their eyes, but Apple was too curious. She opened her fingers and peeked just as Darling bent forward and then came upright quickly, flipping back her long, so-blond-it-was-almost-white hair. As her hair settled around her shoulders, Darling lowered her eyelids halfway and smiled coyly.

And suddenly everything slowed. Apple saw a dust mote trembling in a shaft of morning light, not moving. She tried to lower her hands from her face but they traveled just a couple of inches per minute.

Meanwhile, everyone else who hadn't looked at Darling kept moving at normal speed, which to slow-mo'ed Apple looked like super-speed.

In the time it took Apple to say, "En-chant-ing!" the remaining tasks were finished, the wall and glass cases mended, the helmet tied back on top of the armor, the treasures returned to pedestals, and everything tidy.

Time jumped forward again. Apple and Darling were free from the slow-motion spell just as a herd of mice came scurrying in under the door, squeaking madly.

"They're here!" said Ashlynn. "They're here!"

The door burst open. Helga and Gus led the faculty, including Baba Yaga, Gepetto, Mr. Badwolf, Rumpelstiltskin, Mother Goose, the White Queen, and Maid Marian. Maddie trailed behind, her wrists chained. A troll carried her luggage, which consisted of several hatboxes and a suitcase shaped like a giant nose. And in front of them all was Headmaster Grimm, his face as red as Cerise's cloak.

"What in Ever After is going on here?" he shouted.

Apple blanched. The Treasury was in order. The witnesses were present. They were ready to do the spell and save Maddie. Except Apple had forgotten one pretty essential thing.

Raven. Where was Raven?

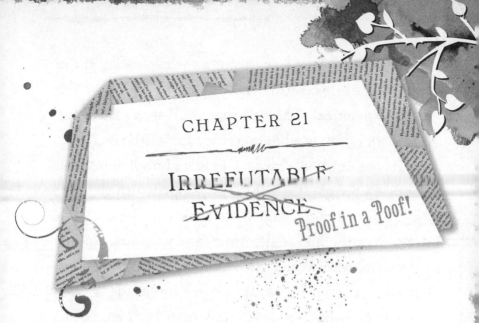

CHAPTER 21

~~IRREFUTABLE~~
~~EVIDENCE~~
Proof in a Poof!

RAVEN'S FINGERTIPS WERE BLISTERED, HER shoulder ached, and her throat was as dry as Milton Grimm's attempts at jokes. After a long night of spell practice, all she wanted was to lie down on her bed, pull the comforter over her head, and play Sleeping Beauty.

But...Maddie.

"No, you're doing it wrong!" said Raven's mother. "I told you, hold it straight."

"I *am* holding it straight," said Raven. "It'd be

easier to get the arrow through the eye socket if the dragon skull was full-sized."

"Be practical. The full-size skull won't fit in the Treasury. You need to practice with it this size."

Raven pulled back Cupid's bowstring. She notched the giant's-hair-arrow, tipped with the pea, and aimed for the empty eye socket in the dragon's skull for the hundredth time. She wobbled. Goblin guts, but was she ever tired. She released the arrow. It missed, bouncing off the skull's forehead.

"If you would just do exactly what I tell you to do, then everything would be better."

"Everything?" Raven lowered the bow. "Like the time you told me to push over that little village girl who was trying to balance on the fountain's edge?"

The queen stuck out her bottom lip, pouting. "A harmless prank. Imagine how funny it would have been when she popped out of the water, drenched and confused!"

"Or the time you sent me to a picnic at the Charming family's palace with a potion you wanted me to pour down their well? Drinking it would have turned them all into cockroaches."

"Again—*funny*. Grow a sense of humor, Raven.

Besides, the potion wasn't even permanent! They would have been back to their normal, goody-goody selves in a year or two. Or three. Probably."

"I didn't want to turn anyone into cockroaches!"

The queen shrugged. "A sense of humor is individual, I suppose. But the past is no excuse for why you're failing now."

The bow felt as heavy as a house. Raven's arms lowered. "This has been a hard day, Mother. And night. The tasks, no sleep, and, worst of all, on Maddie's last day in Ever After I had to ignore her."

"What? You've been upset about that? Ha! You could have talked to Maddie. I made up the silence part. I just wanted you to be focused. Besides, Wonderlandians are too mad to be trusted. You should find yourself more powerful friends."

"You mean...I was mean to her...for...for nothing?" Raven dropped the bow, her fists clenched and sparking with magical energy. "You're *evil*!"

"Why, yes, I am!" said the Evil Queen brightly. "Thank you for noticing. Oh my badness, but you do look simply gorgeous when you're angry. Brightens the eyes and the cheeks! My fairest girl, I'm so proud."

Raven sat on the floor, resting her forehead on

her knees. "I don't care about being fairest. I just...I don't know..."

"You've been away from me too long." The queen breathed on her side of the glass and then rubbed it clean with the sleeve of her scarlet velvet gown. "You've forgotten how wickedly wonderful it is to be evil. Stop wasting your life thinking about *poor widdle Maddie* or *poor widdle anyone* and just do what you want! I didn't raise you to be good and weak, I raised you to be powerful and happy."

"I am happy." Raven kept her head down, embarrassed, as she said quietly, "Happier here than I ever was with you."

Her mother didn't hear. "Don't let the inconsequential fairytales stand in your way! You do what makes you happy, no matter what."

Raven sat upright. "What if what makes you happy hurts other people?"

The queen shrugged. "You think too much, Raven. Look at the natural world—do we cry and whine when a wolf kills a deer? When an eagle takes a hare? Some animals are predators, and they do as they were born to do. You were born to be a predator. You were born to rule."

"I don't want to rule," Raven said. "But…they want me to. The Rebels. They look to me."

"Of course they do." The queen leaned in till her earnest eyes were large in the mirror. "Lead them wherever you want to go, and you'll always have a devoted army at your back."

"I don't know how to do it, Mom," she said. "I'm not like you. I just want…" Raven shrugged.

"Come here, darling," said the queen.

Raven scooted closer to the mirror. Her mother smiled, and Raven wanted nothing more than to be a little girl again, sit on her mother's lap, lean her head against her mother's shoulder, and let her stroke her hair. She lifted her hand but stopped just shy of touching the mirror.

"You are special, Raven," said the queen. "You are more important than most. You are *my* daughter. And I love you."

Part of Raven wanted to take her mother's words like a potion and drink them down, no matter what that potion might do inside her—make her strong, turn her invisible, change her into a cockroach.

"I always wanted you to be proud of me."

"I *am* proud of you, Raven. Why, look at you!

Rebelling against the great Milton Grimm. Ha! You showed him. He wanted you to be evil, and so you are, but what a shock that you don't play by *his* rules."

"But I'm not evil."

"Of course you are! We both rebelled against the system because wonderful, freeing evil courses through our veins."

"No, that doesn't sound right," Raven said. Her mother was so beautiful, her voice as rich as hot chocolate, dark and warm in a mug. The enticing bittersweetness of it made it hard for Raven to think.

"Goodness is weakness. Weak and boring as peas porridge in the pot nine days old. Some actually like it cold, you know. *Imagine.* Now let's get back to work. Practice the incantation again. Remember, you need to speak everyone's name who was in the room, the day and time of the event, and the magic words before *accurately* shooting the arrow through the dragon skull's eye socket."

"I need five, Mom," said Raven, standing. Her thoughts felt as thick in her head as mulberry syrup.

"What? Evil sorceresses don't take five. You

succeed because you're willing to give everything to your craft—everything!"

"Just five minutes."

Raven didn't have enough time for a nap, and she wouldn't risk oversleeping through Maddie's banishment anyway. She just needed to clear her head.

She sat at the keyboard her father had sent and began to play a Tailor Quick tune. Her fingers had stumbled over the string of Cupid's bow, but on the keyboard they knew what to do. Her voice had caught on the words of the incantation, but a song drew them out straight. She played and she sang, and the knotted, snarly mess inside her seemed to settle, as relaxed as Maddie at a tea party.

> *You look around*
> *And you only see what you want to see*
> *You come undone*
> *Trying to be who they want you to be*

Raven sang all three verses, searching for meaning in the words. She held out the final note and played the last chord. It was an odd song, ending on a minor chord halfway through a measure as though it were unfinished. And she liked it. The song felt as true as life.

Raven left the keyboard and sat on the floor in front of the mirror.

"That was..." The Evil Queen looked up as if at clouds, smiling. "That was wicked good."

"Thanks." Raven took a breath. "Here's what I think, Mom. We both rebelled because we wanted to choose our own path, not what destiny dictated. But choice and evil aren't the same. Now that I'm free from my story, I can write my own destiny. I'm sorry, but I won't choose evil. I won't choose your path. I'll find my own."

The Evil Queen opened her mouth as if she would argue, but then she nodded. "And if you change your mind, well, you know where to find me. I'm not going anywhere."

Apple's cuckoo clock cheeped.

Raven jumped to her feet. "Is that the time? Oh, no, I've got to get to the Treasury."

"Go then, and come back and tell me all about it!" Her mother's eyes sparkled as if she truly was excited.

"Okay, I will," said Raven. She stooped to shut

off the mirror but hesitated. The mirror path to the prison was wicked complicated, and having Apple do it for her was kind of a pain. Maybe she could just leave the connection open for now, so she could talk to her mother after the spell—or get extra help if something went wrong. Raven took a second to smile at her mother and said again, "I'll be back soon."

The queen nodded. Her smile seemed truly happy.

Nevermore had curled up on Apple's bed, drooling on her red satin bedspread.

"Nevermore, sweetie, can you get the dragon's skull and follow me?" Raven grabbed the bow, chin hair, and pea, and waved to her mother in the mirror.

"Wish me luck!"

"You don't need luck," said her mother. "You are powerful, clever, and fearless. After all, you are a Queen!"

Raven ran down the stairs, a shrunken-sized Nevermore flying with the shrunken-sized dragon skull in her claws. Raven burst through the Treasury door to find everybody there, staring at Apple.

"Raven!" said Apple. "Here she is. We're ready, Headmaster."

"Whoa, okay," said Raven. "We're *ready* ready? But where's—?"

"Hi, Raven," said Maddie. She couldn't wave. She was standing between Baba Yaga and Gepetto, and her wrists were chained together.

"I'm going to try to help, Maddie," said Raven. "Cross all your crossables for me."

In truth, Raven wasn't feeling all that confident, but Apple was smiling like this was going to be a piece of fig cake.

"Raven," Apple said with warning. "We're not supposed to talk to Maddie."

"It's okay," Raven whispered back. "*She* was lying."

Apple groaned. "You mean I've spent the last several minutes frantically thinking about bunnies for no reason?"

"Bunnies? What?"

"Never mind. Um, ready?" Apple said, still with that confident smile.

"Yes, okay," said Raven.

"I did not give you permission to—" Milton Grimm began.

"Please, Headmaster Grimm?" said Apple. "You

said only Irrefutable Evidence could pardon Maddie, and we're prepared to show you just that."

"Raven Queen isn't capable of casting a level thirty-eight spell." He shook his head. "You have precisely one minute, Your Majesty, and then I must ask you not to interfere with this serious school business."

"Thank you, Headmaster," Apple said. She took Raven's hands and made the most direct of direct eye contact Raven had ever experienced. Apple's confident smile twinkled, brilliant, inspiring. "You can do this, Raven Queen."

And for the first time, Raven believed that she could. "Okay," she said. Her heart was thumping, slammed unexpectedly with a tremendous amount of hope.

She spared a glance to admire the clean and ordered Treasury and then asked everyone to stand back by the door. Nevermore placed the dragon skull before them.

"Everyone who was here that night, please look at the skull," said Raven.

She spoke their names, the date and time of the event, and then the words of the incantation, hoping that they were all correct. Her mother had to relay them to her through riddles.

"'I call down evidence of pure truth,'" she intoned. "'I call up the spirits of memory. Rewind, replay, speak up, stand out. Through the eye of a monster, let the past dance again!'"

Raven secured the pea on the tip of the hair, drew back the bowstring, and aimed straight. She released. The arrow went through the eye socket.

Out of the empty eye, pink smoke billowed, engulfing the room. When it overtook Raven, she could smell nothing. It was all illusion. The smoke pulled back into a ball spiked like the claws of some amorphous beast. The smoke claws lengthened, pointing at the eyes of Raven, Apple, Maddie, and all the other students. Then the smoke broke into a hundred pieces and took on colors and shapes. And suddenly Sparrow Hood was running into the Treasury.

Raven almost yelled at him to stay back, but then the real Sparrow, who was still standing back by the door, said, "That's one handsome kid!"

Raven was watching a ghost, a memory: It looked like Sparrow, but his colors were slightly washed out, his body a little transparent. He was talking, but no noise came out. His Merry Men followed, and Sparrow began taking items and putting them into his pockets.

It was like watching a silent play or an eerily real three-dimensional movie. The smoky memories of the other students entered the Treasury, shouting silently to one another, romping around.

Kitty appeared suddenly in front of Ashlynn, who was startled and bumped into Hunter. Hunter backed up, the sword in his hand cracking the glass in a display case. Sparrow nocked an arrow, aiming at King Arthur's shield on the wall. Dexter flying on a broomstick wobbled to avoid the arrow and bumped into the helmet of a giant's suit of armor. Sparrow's arrow grazed against the falling helmet, knocking the arrow off course and into the cracked display case, breaking the glass further.

At the same moment, Blondie tripped over the cape she was wearing, knocking into Lizzie, who stumbled into Duchess, who was puppeting Humphrey Dumpty on Pinocchio's strings. Duchess glided out of the way, letting Lizzie bang into the display case. The tiny unicorn inside fell off its pedestal.

The Merry Men had found the instruments, and one played a horn so loudly the sound lengthened the glass break even more, just as Briar and Cedar skipped by. Helga tossed a jug to Gus. It nearly hit Cedar, but Dexter caught it in time. His elbow grazed the case, and the unicorn fell all the way out. Daring moved to heroically help his sister Darling over the broken glass and nudged the unicorn with his foot, sending it across the floor.

Almost every person's foot touched the unicorn as he or she ran around the Treasury, unknowingly knocking it this way and that until it came to rest before the giant helmet just as Maddie entered.

She never even touched the unicorn as she picked a few things off the floor, stuffed them in her pockets, and climbed atop the helmet. She lifted her arms happily. The image froze and disappeared.

For a few moments, everyone was quiet.

"Baba Yaga—?" the headmaster began.

"It was the real deal," Baba Yaga said, tasting the air. She turned her stony gaze on Raven and raised one gray eyebrow. "An Irrefutable Evidence spell. Impossible to fake."

The headmaster stared at Raven, too, eyes

blazing, as if he didn't know whether to be angry or afraid.

"It seems to me," Mr. Badwolf growled, "that if you were to banish those responsible for the broken Uni Cairn, you would need to banish nearly every student in this room *except* Madeline Hatter."

"And all those destinies would be banished with them," said Apple.

The headmaster's frown was so severe his mustache tilted down with it so that he seemed to have two frowns.

"But…she was clearly stealing items from the Treasury," he said, "and that alone—"

"Um, pardon me, Headmaster Grimm," said Apple, "but perhaps you could ask her why she took those things?"

He blew out his cheeks but nodded and turned to Maddie. "Why?" he said.

"I thought it was the Swappersnatch Gyre, of course!" said Maddie. "Everyone stealing for fun, and all the hiding and hunting and finding that follows. In Wonderland we do it every spring."

Lizzie Hearts nodded. "I declare Madeline Hatter is correct!"

"It's how we play," Kitty said with a smile just as large as the headmaster's frown.

"In that case—" Headmaster Grimm said.

"Finally!" Baba Yaga interrupted. She pointed a crooked finger at Maddie, and the chains sizzled and fell from her wrists. "I've got better things to do than banish a little girl to that pirate-infested island. My office has been exceedingly grumpy for some reason. Excuse me, I have to go soothe a walking cottage."

Baba Yaga stormed out.

The cottage...

Raven began to think something important, but the thought was chased from her head by a furious-faced Headmaster Grimm.

"Just how did you manage to cast a level thirty-eight spell?" he asked, his shoulders tense and rising to his ears.

"My mom taught me," she said truthfully. "After all, she wants me to grow up to be just like her."

The headmaster's eyes narrowed, but he'd have to assume her mother taught her the spell years ago. After all, Raven had no access to a mother locked away in a spell-repellent cell.

"Hmph," he said and stalked off.

And suddenly Raven was jounced by a quick and hard hug.

"I knew it!" said Maddie. "I just knew you were still my best friend till The End."

"There were a few times this week I did think it was actually The End," said Raven. "I'm sorry I couldn't tell you. I thought silence was a condition of the spell. I know you must have felt like a pile of giant toenail clippings when I ignored you."

For some reason, Apple shuddered.

"Think no more gloomy fussy gussy thoughts about it." Maddie hugged her again. "Thank you."

Everyone began congratulating Maddie, Sparrow loudly taking all the credit for her miraculous rescue.

Raven received another surprise hug, this time from Apple.

"I was *confident*, Raven!" she said. "So many times the last couple of days, I worried that I didn't know how to be a leader anymore. But I smiled, and I looked, and I had ideas, and I led them! And you were so amazing—the spell, and—Wow! We did it! Maddie is safe!"

"The Treasury looks amazing," said Raven. "You seriously rock for pulling it off."

"We both seriously, enchantingly, perfectly rock," said Apple. Her voice dropped lower. "You know, there were moments I was so afraid *she* was just trying to trick us. I had a plan B prepared for when the spell backfired and caused some horrible havoc. But it worked!"

"What was your plan B?"

"Hmm?" said Apple. "Oh, subvert the banishment route through the wishing well. I thought maybe I could hack into the travel app and change her route from Neverland to my home castle. Watching Humphrey on the Mirror Network gave me some ideas. It wasn't a certain thing, but no worries! Now I don't have to even try!"

"And it worked, even though we did get a lot of help," said Raven.

"Yeah, no offense, but your mom's advice about not depending on anyone but yourself was kind of evil."

Raven laughed.

"We would have completely failed without all our friends!" said Apple. "The Mad Hatter, Ashlynn, Gala, the pixies—"

"Cedar and Nevermore—"

"—Briar—"

"—and Cerise," said Raven. "And Cupid, too."

"Ooh, and Humphrey and Dexter—"

"*Her*..."

"And then practically *everyone* helped me with the Treasury," said Apple.

"I know she's evil, but she seemed like she really did want me to succeed," Raven whispered. "She's waiting to hear about the victory."

Apple froze. "You didn't leave the mirror on, did you? Surely, you at least put it in standby mode."

"Should I have? I mean, she can't escape. Oh, I was thinking earlier. Baba Yaga's cottage? We didn't need to use all the ingredients for the spell after all. The egg, nor the tea, either, now that I think of it. It's funny that—"

Raven stopped. Apple seized her hand. Her own was ice cold.

"The tea and the egg," Apple whispered. "They're still in our room? With the mirror?"

Raven suddenly wanted a weapon in hand. She grabbed something long, skinny, and gold from a nearby pedestal. Apple was still gripping her other hand, and she pulled. Together, they ran.

They ran through the middle of the crowd of students and muddle of faculty. They ran down the hall, their heels clacking against stones.

"Will o' the wisps!" Apple said. "How did I not realize? Will o' the wisps move between worlds, see? So drinking will o' the wisp tea imbues someone with the ability to cross over borders!"

"Borders like the one between our world and mirror prison," said Raven. "And the cottage! It's bigger on the inside than on the out. Even big enough for a woman to climb inside. Besides, it's an enchanted cottage, born with chicken legs, inherently free range. No foundation can hold it, and no prison would confine it. Baba Yaga told me she began using it as her office as a protection against capture by evil sorceresses like my mother!"

"So if the hutling hatched and drank the will o' the wisps tea…"

"It might be empowered to cross over through our viewing mirror and into actual mirror prison," said Raven as they raced up some stairs. "And once inside…"

"Your mother would be able to climb inside the

hutling, and its natural freedom would carry them out of the prison!"

"And back into our world."

"We'd be banished for meddling with one of the Great Glass Prisons!" said Apple.

"Forget that," said Raven. "Think what my mother would do to Ever After!"

Apple sped up.

They slammed open their dorm door.

From inside the mirror, the Evil Queen was chanting. The words came out as nonsense, and with each one spoken she winced as if feeling the stings of the spell repellent. When she saw Raven and Apple, she began chanting faster.

A long, thin line like steam trailed from the mirror through the room and into the cup of tea. The heat from the tea was warming the egg, steamy tendrils rising, wrapping around its bright spotted shell. Already there were cracks.

"Get the egg!" Raven said.

Raven and Apple ran forward. Raven leaped to tackle it, but while she was still in midleap, the egg burst. A cottage the size of a large dog wobbled forward on its thin chicken legs, leaving Raven to land on a pile of shell shards. The hutling shook itself, made a raspy screech, and started to run.

"Get it!" Raven said. "Stop it!"

The cottage sniffed, inhaling with an open door. It trotted over to the cup of tea and with a peck from its front door took a sip from the cup.

"No!" said Apple. She'd pulled the satin bedspread from her bed and ran at the hutling, leaping onto it.

"Ha-ha!" said Apple, trapping the little cottage beneath the bedspread.

A rip. The hutling's door gnawed a hole through the cloth and leaped through.

The queen's chanting had stopped. Now she was calling.

"Here, boy! Come here, boy! That's a good hutling. Look at what a good hutling! I have some yummy treats for you! Just come through the mirror."

The hutling paused as if to listen. It started toward the mirror.

"No, you don't," said Raven, intercepting it. She was still holding whatever she'd grabbed from the Treasury, and she swung it, missing the hutling.

"Raven!" said the Evil Queen. "Stop it at once!"

"Sorry, Mom," said Raven.

The queen took a breath and her voice softened. "Raven, darling, why can't you help your own mother?"

Like its parent, the hutling did not like to be chased. It squawked and ran faster and faster, dodging Apple and Raven. They leaped at it, landing in a dog pile on its roof, but the little hut kept running, leaving the girls clinging to its rain gutters. And still the hutling ran. It was small, but it was as solid as a full-grown house, and in its speed, it left destruction in its wake. Apple's bed was demolished. Her dresser reduced to firewood. Wardrobe knocked over with a crash. Clothing ripped and flying in the air like confetti.

"No," Apple said with a sob.

Next the cottage dragged them through Raven's part of the room, destroying everything it touched. Raven winced at the loss of her bed and wardrobe, but ahead was her vanity and its hidden keyboard.

"No! Stop!"

Raven dug her heels into the floor, trying desperately to slow the hutling, but it barreled ahead. A crash and a musical twang, and Raven's beautiful keyboard was nothing more than scrap wood and metal.

Raven let go, rolling into the keyboard debris. A single sob escaped her lips. Then she turned her gaze to her mother, still calling from the mirror.

"Come here, boy! Come on!"

"*No!*" Raven yelled.

Her mother startled, the words drying in her mouth.

Raven didn't dare touch the glass but felt around the back of the mirror, trying to find an off switch.

"Don't let go, Apple!" Raven yelled.

"Ack, ow, uhhh…" Apple said, dragging behind the hutling.

Raven was about to drop the tool to better feel for the off switch, but then she recognized what she was really holding in her hand: her mother's own scepter that had been on display in the Treasury. It had no magic and yet was a symbol of queenly power—heavy, golden, magnificent.

Raven walked to the front mirror and raised the scepter up.

"No!" Her mother's beautiful face twisted with rage. "I thought you were finally evil, Raven!"

"You took away Maddie's Wonderland," said Raven. "I'm sorry, Mom. I respect your right to make your own path, but when your choices hurt people, you have to face the consequences. You need to stay where you are."

"I love you!" her mother shouted.

Part of Raven's heart cracked, but she gripped the heavy gold stick even tighter.

The mirror was the only unbroken thing left in the room. Raven smashed it with her mother's scepter.

"Me too," she whispered.

CHAPTER 22

Musically! MADDIE PESTERS THE NARRATOR

Narrator! Do you know where Raven went? And Apple? They were here a minute ago, but I can't hear you telling their story anymore, so they must be gone.

Yes, they left, Maddie.

Just a sec, Cedar, I'm talking to the Narrator. Um, what was that?

I said they left, but I'm sure they'll be back.

They've been so...so...just so wonderlandiful! I wish I could give them a splendiferous thank-you gift. I know what Raven might like—a girls' day: tea party, shopping, and going to listen to that new band that's playing at Looking Glass Beach tonight. But I don't know what Apple would like.

Well…

You know, don't you? Oh, please, tell me, please please please please please…

I can't, Maddie! I took a Narrator's oath not to interfere!

That's okay. I understand. I guess I'll just stand here and sing all three hundred and sixty-four verses of the Wonderlandian song "If I Snoodled on a Poodle" while I try to think of the perfect gift for Apple. Oh, if I snoodled, snoodled, snoodled on a poodle with a noodle, would you groodle, groodle, groodle with an oodle of hot strudel—

You really are a clever thing, you know that. Look, if you go to their dorm room, you might get a good idea on your own. But you didn't hear that from me, okay?

Narrator, I'm going to give you a legible kiss. Smooch!!!

CHAPTER 23

HAPPILY EVER AFTERS

APPLE KEPT CLINGING TO THE HUTLING. The roof was made of thatch, or fur, really. She could feel the warm skin beneath. Its windows opened and shut like eyelids, its hard, round body straining to keep running while pulling Apple along for the ride. Even so, it hadn't slowed at all and showed no intention of stopping. Apple imagined herself dragging behind the tiny cottage all day, and the next, and years from now, still holding on, bumping along behind. It had already destroyed her room. Perhaps it would tear apart all of Ever After, too.

Apple whimpered. But Raven had said, "Don't let go," and she didn't want to let Raven down. Or Maddie. Or anyone, ever.

So she clung on.

She heard a *crash* as Raven broke the mirror. A moment later the small cottage in Apple's arms began to rise into the air. Apple swallowed a scream and let go, dropping to the floor.

"The levitation spell worked!" Raven said, her hands held up, glowing purple, her brow tight with concentration. "I can't believe it didn't backfire, but I wouldn't trust it to last long."

The cottage hung from nothing, its little chicken legs fighting the air, its door and window blinds wide open.

"We need a leash," Apple said. "Oh wait, I've got it!"

Apple ran to her dresser, but in its place was a pile of wood and heaps of clothes torn and full of splinters. Apple whimpered again. She kept her back to Raven so that her roommate wouldn't see the ridiculous tears welling in her eyes.

It's just stuff, Apple told herself. *It doesn't matter really. You don't have to be perfect, and neither does . . . neither does your . . . your perfect, beautiful room!*

Apple wiped her eyes, trolled through the mess, and pulled out a woven yellow scarf. "It was made from Holly's hair! Super-strong, magical, the perfect leash."

Apple tied it around the middle of the cottage, and at once the hutling calmed. Kept from running, it seemed to relax. Its blinds lowered in its front windows, its legs buckled, and it began to snooze, its front door clacking gently against its threshold.

Apple plucked the hutling from the air, and Raven released the levitation spell.

"This little fella needs to go home," said Apple.

"Yeah, wherever that home might be running around at the moment," said Raven.

Through the castle, Apple carried the hutling under a torn piece of her bedspread, petting its thatch head. It was just a newborn cottage, after all.

Outside, Raven tracked Baba Yaga's office to the sports fields. Apple set the hutling down. The girls ran behind a tree and watched as the parent cottage discovered the baby. There was much squawking and slamming of front doors. Soon the big cottage was running around the field as if in pure joy, the hutling nuzzling down on its parent's roof, cozy beside the chimney.

"You know, when I took that egg," said Raven, "I didn't think it through, how there was a baby inside who would miss its parent. I guess there are a lot of things I don't think through."

Apple nodded. Her queenly instinct perked up, and she opened her mouth to offer a poetic speech about a homecoming, the bond between parent and child abodes, the beauty of a baby domicile, or some such. But an image of their wrecked dorm room flashed in her mind. Her chin quivered, warning her that if she spoke, she would cry. It was a silly thing to be so upset. After all, Maddie was free! And the Evil Queen wasn't! Still...her grandmother's antique chair...the cuckoo clock the village children had given her...the red dress her mother had stitched without any bird help at all...all her precious things...

They walked back in silence. Apple was too ashamed of herself to say anything, but Raven put a warm hand on Apple's shoulder, as if she knew.

They stopped before the door to their dorm room, Apple hesitating, uncertain if she could face it again.

"Apple," Raven started.

The door opened, and Maddie came bursting out, shutting the door behind her.

"Ah-ha!" she said. "I heard the Narrator say that Apple was hesitating, so I knew you were near. So the Narrator may have *accidentally* let slip that I should come to your room, and when I saw the mess, I thought, well, that's not like Apple White! I mean sure, Raven is known to use the floor as a temporary holding place for dirty clothes and hextbooks and items of relative value. But Apple? Never. So I had an idea...."

Maddie opened the door. She wasn't alone.

Ashlynn sat on the floor behind a pile of Raven's and Apple's clothing, stitching up a rip in one of Apple's skirts. Beside her a family of raccoons worked, peering at the tears a pair of chicken feet had made in skirts and blouses, threaded needles held in their nimble gray fingers.

Cupid and Cedar were examining the furniture. Cedar seemed to have an excellent eye for wood, and she'd hold the broken pieces of a dresser together while Cupid ran the tip of her arrow down the fracture, mending it.

"A keyboard is tough to fix, but I'll do my best," said Cupid. "Most wood seems to mend well. And glass, too, so that mirror shouldn't be a problem—"

"Uh…you can leave that mirror broken," said Raven.

Apple nodded. *Just in case*, she thought.

Hunter was fixing Apple's bed, Lizzie making a new side table out of stacked cards that magically held together strong enough to support her lamp.

"Apple, I am here," Daring said, pausing to flash a smile so brilliant Apple's eyes started to water all over again. Then his arms dropped to his sides. "Though I'm not exactly clear what I'm doing. If you had a dragon that needed slaying, I could be courageous and victorious for you. But cleaning up…"

"It's okay," said Apple, "being here is enough."

"I'm here, too!" said Briar, coming in for a running embrace. "Wow, I don't know what happened in here, but I know my Apple pie, and I know this mess must be *killing* you. Don't worry, we've got your back. Look at this!" Briar held up a red-and-white color-blocked dress. "This used to be two dresses, and they were too messed up for Ashlynn to fix. But I designed a new dress out of the scraps."

"Enchanting!" said Apple, holding it up to her front.

Dexter came from Raven's part of the room holding an armload of clothes. His face turned bright red, and he adjusted his glasses, dropping the clothing.

"Raven! Sorry, I didn't see you come in. I was just helping Ashlynn, I didn't mean to touch your private stuff. But I did happen to see you have the new Lady Yaga album. Did you know she's actually Baba Yaga's niece?"

Raven and Dexter started sorting clothing while talking music. Briar helped Melody Piper set up her stuff to DJ the restoration party and then began hauling throw pillows in from her own room to decorate Apple's restored bed. One of the pillows bore an ironed-on photo of One Reflection. Blondie began placing everything back just right. Ginger brought in a fresh batch of cookies for a snack. Cerise ran in the door, bringing glue and new paint. Kitty disappeared and reappeared here and there, returning things to their places.

"Apple?" said Holly, plucking out single hairs from her head for Ashlynn and the raccoons to use as threads. "Hey, I just wanted you to know, after you left Buff Castle, I talked to a servant there—I think his name was Plum or something?—and I told him what you'd said. And he took your advice and arranged it so the castle bought produce from both farmers. One of them was so happy he cried."

"Thanks, Holly," said Apple. She felt near some happy crying herself.

Maddie gripped Apple in a sudden hug. "I smintered your balcony throne, and you still saved me. Thank you."

"Of course! Hey, Maddie, my worthy co-president, I want to make some changes at the school so what happened to you can't occur again. Will you help me draft a proposal regarding the proper conduct of a student trial?"

"Absotively, my distinguished co-president," said Maddie.

Raven crouched down by Cedar, who was examining the kindling the hutling had made of Apple's wardrobe. Raven took a deep breath, as if afraid to speak what was on her tongue.

"Cedar, I know you can't tell me a lie, and so I've been afraid to ask you, but I need to know. Is all the bad stuff that happened after Legacy Day my fault?"

Cedar winced, but she said, "Some of it. None of us are hermits living alone on a mountain. Everything we do affects other people. And you did a big thing. So, yeah, a lot of the chaos and anxiety and craziness the last couple of days was set in motion by what you did."

Raven nodded. "That's what I was afraid of."

"That doesn't mean what you did was necessarily wrong, and it doesn't mean you're to blame for the choices everyone else made, but you did affect it all in a big way, no question. Sorry, Raven."

Raven stood up and faced the room. "Hey, everybody, can I say something?"

Melody turned down the volume.

"I didn't want this to be my fault," said Raven. "But some of it is. Pretending otherwise is acting too much like my mom, who did whatever she wanted and took no notice of anyone she hurt along the way. I'm sorry that the backlash of my decision hurt many of you."

She glanced at Apple. Apple smiled back.

"I haven't changed my mind about not signing the book," said Raven. "But I know that many of you are feeling lost about what to do now—follow your destiny or write your own? I don't know all the answers, but I'd like to lead a support group, I guess. We can meet here once a week. Anyone interested could come talk about destiny—to follow it or not—and if not, we can talk about what to do now. You know, lean on one another a bit, figure this out together."

"I'll be there," said Cedar.

"So will I," said Hunter.

Several other people voiced support as well.

"What a charming idea, Raven!" said Apple. "I'll come to your support group, too, if that's all right, just to lend a Royal voice to the discussion."

"Of course," said Raven. "Your perspective will be an asset."

"Thank you," said Apple. "I'm eager to appreciate your perspective better. For instance, I understand that you value choice over destiny. But what if my choice *is* my destiny?"

"Um, okay, you can still make that choice."

"I'm not sure," said Apple. "If you don't play your part in our story, how do I get my Happily Ever After?"

"That might still happen," said Raven, "even without me."

"But I think the Snow White tale is worth fighting for. All our stories are worth fighting for. If we don't retell them, they fade away."

"The stories we write for ourselves by how we live our lives might be even better than our parents' stories," Raven said.

"Why risk the loss of all the old stories?" asked Apple.

"Can't we retell them without living them?"

"Not according to Headmaster Grimm. Besides, living them is a great privilege, as well as a guarantee for a particular life. Without destiny, there's no guarantee of any Happily Ever After, not just for me but for all of us."

"*With* destiny, many of us were guaranteed an unhappy ever after," Raven said. "Now at least we can choose our own lives."

Apple's heart was pounding. "But with choice there aren't any guarantees. Maybe *no one* will get a Happily Ever After now. Why gamble away the ones we had in exchange for possibly none at all?"

"Because before there was *no* chance that everyone would get that happy ending," said Raven, her voice rising. "Now at least there's some chance."

"A chance?" Apple said. "You're willing to risk all those happy destinies for just a chance? How do you know if anyone will get a—"

"I don't!" Raven shouted. "No one knows! This is life and we just live it and hope for the best!"

Raven was even paler than usual, her eyes a bright purple, her hands clenched. Apple supposed she looked fierce: evil and powerful and scary even. But Apple kept picturing her as she looked hanging onto that hutling for dear life, hair wild, eyes wide, bumping along as they crashed through the room.

And Apple giggled.

Raven looked incredulous. She opened her mouth as if to shout back, but instead a laugh came out.

And then Apple and Raven were holding each other, exhausted from their sleepless night, and laughing so hard Apple thought she might split her seams. The more they laughed the harder it came, till Apple's stomach hurt and eyes streamed. It had been a really long day.

Everyone was watching them, unsure if they'd lost their minds. Which was even funnier. And they laughed some more.

Apple wheezed, trying to get the laugh under

control. Raven managed to stop first, though she was hiccuping now. Apple took a deep breath.

"We both want the same thing," Apple said both to Raven and to everyone in the room.

"Yeah, Happily Ever Afters for ourselves and our friends," said Raven.

"We just disagree how to get that."

Cedar shook her head. "I still don't know what choice I should make."

"I think that's okay, Cedar," said Raven.

"It most definitely is," said Apple. "We don't have to decide what our entire lives will be right now."

"We're still in high school, for Grandma's sake," said Cerise.

"Right, we have plenty of time to make up our minds," said Ashlynn.

"Or change them," said Hunter. He cast a shy smile toward Ashlynn. "And this is a good place to be while I figure stuff out. I mean, all my friends are here. And the people I care a lot about."

"I care about the people here, too," Ashlynn said, her eyes on her stitching. "A lot. And if we don't have to decide everything right now—"

"Off with their heads!" Lizzie suddenly shouted.

Apple stared. "Why?"

"Oops, I meant to say, 'Here, here,'" Lizzie said. "Sometimes the wrong words come out."

"Ooh, sometimes the wrong words can be the right words," said Maddie, who was collecting loose feathers and stuffing them back into a pillow. "Let's play a game. At the same time, everybody say the first word that pops into your mind. One, two, three!"

"Freedom," said Raven.

"Family," said Cerise.

"Color," said Cedar.

"Fun," said Briar.

"Handsome," said Daring.

"Mice," said Kitty.

"Doors," said Blondie.

"Croquet," said Lizzie.

"Rhythm," said Melody.

"Snickerdoodles," said Ginger.

"Whistles," said Maddie.

"Love," said Cupid. And Ashlynn. And Hunter. And Dexter, too. They looked at one another and laughed.

"Friends," said Apple.

Blondie passed out bowls of porridge sweetened

with a great deal of honey. Maddie produced a tea party seemingly out of her hat. Melody played a jam with a really great beat.

Apple's dorm room was still a shambles. Some things would never be fixed, not completely. But there was porridge and tea, and friends that were trying. And Apple thought, *Everything doesn't have to be perfect right now. For the moment, trying is enough.*

She sipped her tea and felt warm. She found a hanger and hung up the first mended dress. Then Briar pulled her into the center of the room, and Apple took a short break from working so she could dance.

Also Very Evil
EPILOGUE

NESTLED BETWEEN THE EPIC PEAKS, the jabberwocky flexed its wings. It was delighted to be free of its tiny glass prison, and doubly delighted to have found delicious bears to eat on its way up the mountain.

But things were wrong in this slithy, little land. The sun moved in a straight line, and things remained a certain size and shape no matter how the jabberwock looked or screamed at them. Its intention had been to find a spot or a clime, an angle or a time where rabbit holes were large and the jabberwock could be made small. It would have burrowed inside, eaten the rabbits, and slept, unnoticed, until it felt right again. But for all it spun and ducked and searched and clucked, it remained fearsomely large. For all it dug and flapped and poked and slapped, the mountains did not become molehills and the trees of the forest did not become broccoli.

Clearly, this was *not* Wonderland.

What a wretched and mimsy place the Great Manxome Jabberwocky had been released into, and it did not like it at all. Its foods of choice were misplaced and every Rule of Nothing was broken. Things would need to be done. Iron, tree, and stone would need to be torn and rent and broken and bent until this place became home or until home became this place.

Lights flashed in the valley below, and the jabberwock snaked its long neck around to look. This was a land of creatures of skin and fur. But no other wocks or jubjub birds or even a single tove. And so many two-legs that walked like Alice and Hatterfolk.

Yes. There had been Hatterkin spied at its escape from the Uni Cairn. And the scent of The Cat and sounds of the Card Queen, too. There were pieces of Wonderland here. Pieces it would move, poke, and prod until the Dull Wrongness of this place transformed into the Splendid Wrongness of Wonderland.

The jabberwocky yawned with a mouth the size of a castle gate. First, it would have a nap. Then it would find the Hatterkin. What had it been called?

The beast twitched and then closed its eyes with a smile. "Maddie," it whispered, and began to snore.

ACKNOWLEDGMENTS

It was an honor to return to Ever After High! Ogre-sized hugs to the creative team at Mattel who brought this world to life, including Cindy Ledermann, Lara Dalian, Emily Kelly, Christine Kim, Robert Rudman, Julia Phelps, and Talia Rodgers. Thanks for letting me join your storytelling party.

Courtly bows and rakish winks to the Little, Brown team, including Erin Stein, Connie Hsu, Andrew Smith, Melanie Chang, Victoria Stapleton, Christine Ma, Christina Quintero, Tim Hall, Mara

Lander, Jenn Corcoran, and Jonathan Lopes. My, what a crew! Surely you qualify as a coven.

This book would not exist without the wicked skills of Dean Hale, my partner in crime, punishment, storytelling, and everything else. All the good parts are yours, baby.

ABOUT THE AUTHOR

New York Times bestselling author SHANNON HALE knew at age ten that it was her destiny to become a writer. She has quested deep into fairy tales in such enchanting books as *Ever After High: The Storybook of Legends*, *The Goose Girl*, *Book of a Thousand Days*, *Rapunzel's Revenge*, and Newbery Honor recipient *Princess Academy*. With the princely and valiant writer Dean Hale, Shannon coauthored four charming children, who are free to follow their own destinies. Just so long as they get to bed on time.